I0795585

A WRITING MARRIAGE

Also by Lori Carlson-Hijuelos

A Path to the World

Cool Salsa

Red Hot Salsa

The Sunday Tertulia

A Stitch in Air

Burnt Sugar

A WRITING MARRIAGE

LORI CARLSON-HIJUELOS

with excerpts from
Blue Antiquity
by Oscar Hijuelos

A REGALO PRESS BOOK

A Writing Marriage:
With Excerpts from Blue Antiquity
© 2026 by Lori Carlson-Hijuelos
All Rights Reserved

ISBN: 979-8-88845-178-6
ISBN (eBook): 979-8-88845-179-3

Cover design by Conroy Accord
Interior design and composition, Greg Johnson, Textbook Perfect

Publishing Team
Founder and Publisher: Gretchen Young
Managing Editor: Caitlin Burdette
Production Manager: Kate Harris
Production Editor: Rachel Paul

This is a work of nonfiction. All people, locations, events, and situations are portrayed to the best of the author's memory.

As part of the mission of Regalo Press, a donation is being made to the American Heart Association, as chosen by the author. Find out more about this organization at https://www.heart.org/en/.

This book, as well as any other Regalo Press publications, may be purchased in bulk quantities at a special discounted rate. Contact orders@regalopress.com for more information.

No part of this book may be reproduced, stored in a retrieval system, or transmitted by any means without the written permission of the author and publisher.

Regalo Press
New York • Nashville
regalopress.com

Published in the United States of America
1 2 3 4 5 6 7 8 9 10

For Mom

Contents

A Note About This Book ix

Prelude 1
A Library in a Church 4
A Brief Interlude .7
Spanish 10
Imagery and Influence 19
A Writing Marriage 22
Books 30
Divergent Backgrounds 37
A Little Christmas. 45
Sudden Fame, Consequences 54
Wrapped in Music. .60
Rosemary. 65
Tagine. 71
Routines and Breaking Them 76
Winter Weather 97
It is Spring 102
Privacy and Respect. 113
Space 118
Conversation 125
Summer. 151
Insomnia 156
The Radiant Life 159
Postlude 164

Acknowledgments 166
About the Authors 170

A Note About This Book

A FEW MONTHS AFTER MY HUSBAND, Oscar Hijuelos, died in 2013, I began thinking about how to handle the bulk of his extraordinary archive (a part of which was already at Columbia University's Rare Book and Manuscript Library). Finding the appropriate repository for his voluminous papers was one of four main objectives I wished to accomplish for the future custody of his work—a multifaceted and complex mission.

The truth was I could not enter Oscar's studio, where he kept most of his professional belongings and manuscripts, because the grief I felt was so debilitating and relentless it prevented me from facing his expansive energy: Oscar might have been taken physically from this earth, but the unseen magnetic element of his soul was as powerful as ever.

I decided that Oscar's archives would remain in his studio for only the professionals to peruse and arrange.

I would wait until I was able to read his papers without falling apart.

Eventually, to my delight, his archives did find the perfect home at the Library of Congress.

When I was informed there were some 2,000 pages of a novel in several boxes among the many, I was relieved and curious. The novel had two titles: *So Imagined Mercado* and *Blue Antiquity*. I knew that Oscar had decided on the latter as the final choice because we had discussed, quite often over the years, which of the two was more compelling. I preferred *Blue Antiquity*, and, in the end, so did he.

Oscar had shown me pages of this searing fiction periodically. It was a work that he kept writing while crafting his other books. In fact, he had begun the opus in the late 1980s, as sketches and detailed notes, when he became a fellow at the American Academy in Rome after winning the Rome Prize for his first novel, *Our House in the Last World*. What I had not realized was the size of the manuscript, the scope, and the fullness of his thinking about it. I simply hadn't known that it was so substantive.

One day, quite a few years after his passing, Oscar's agent and mine, Jennifer Lyons, wrote to tell me that she had found a section—the very first one hundred pages or so—of *Blue Antiquity* that he had polished, perfected, and had sent to her to read before showing them to his editor, Gretchen Young. He had released these pages by email to Jennifer just a few weeks prior to his death. Gretchen, at the time, was working at Grand Central Publishing/Hachette Book Group as senior editor and VP.

When Gretchen heard from my agent that I was writing about my life with Oscar, she asked to see some of my pages. Jennifer also asked her to look at Oscar's work in progress from *Blue Antiquity*. She graciously accepted to do so and started to read both of our offerings immediately.

Gretchen realized, soon thereafter, that *Blue Antiquity* referred to the culmination of Oscar's artistic vision and was also an allusion to ancient history and the beginnings of civilization. This capstone novel—in effect a summation of what my husband believed about life, love, death, and eternity—centers on a scholar who is facing his mortality. He senses that his health is seriously failing, while keeping this knowledge to himself.

More specifically, *Blue Antiquity* suggests the fullness of Oscar's philosophical and spiritual development as articulated by the protagonist, Victor Mercado, an historian and classicist whose dissertation, *The Pagan Roots of Christianity*, awards him an appointment in the Department of History and Classics at a small liberal arts school by the name of Angerona College. Mercado has a reputation for specializing in the life of Christ. In short, he is an academic who has achieved a certain level of success. His ethnic identity, like Oscar's, is that of the son of Cuban immigrants. His passion—and the source of his intellectual verve—is working on archaeological digs. In the following excerpt from *Blue Antiquity,* Oscar could have been talking about himself instead of his fictional counterpart:

In his twenty-five years of European excavations, he had seen mostly everything of antiquity. He knew what it was like to sleep in fields under the stars, on the decks of overnight ferries, on the hard seats of tobacco fume filled train cars; on sea walls, on docks, on the rooftops of one- dollar-a-night Turkish pensions, and in the waiting rooms of dead-end train stations in the middle of nowhere. He knew the crisp air of the Roman forum at seven in the morning, the monuments and temples of that great graveyard of stone, riddled with ghosts. He had battled the mud, the thickets, the hard unyielding ground, the burning stones, the rising templates of heat, the stinging black flies of Turkey, the monotony of repetitious tasks, the inquiries of pushy German tourists peering over the barricades into the trenches dug around the temple of the Vestal Virgins in the Forum, the backaches, pulled tendons and sore feet that come with those exertions. Since his younger days, he was good at yielding a pick and shovel and at judging the weight, in stones and rocks, that he could tolerate while pushing a wheel barrel up a trench plank. He could determine just how high a mound of excavation debris should rise, and of where and how thickly to spread his *porcelana*, the greenish volcanic *"Kilroy-was-here"* sediment that archeologists laid down as a demarcation fill at excavation's end. He knew the workings of surveyors' instruments to ascertain an elevation, and, as well, how to take core samples of the soil, and to date their levels, as might a geoarchaeologist.

The cultural upbringing, hobbies, avocations, passions, and beliefs of Mercado and Oscar are virtually the same.

As I ruminated on the pages before me in my living room, I realized that Oscar was Mercado to a very large degree. I also discerned that if Oscar were alive to finish this work, it would be among his crowning achievements.

After reading both my proposal and Oscar's pages, Gretchen got in touch with Jennifer and said she would like to publish my memoir. She also informed Jennifer that she had a position at another house, Post Hill Press, and that she was going to start an imprint there by the name of Regalo (which means "gift" in Spanish and Italian). She had some thoughts about my pages that she wished to share, and she asked to talk to me about her ideas.

The book you have in your hands is the result of that conversation: My husband's words are woven together with mine. I have chosen excerpts from *Blue Antiquity* to harmonize with and expand upon select recollections of our relationship. It has been more than a writing exercise for me. It has been an unexpected pilgrimage to the heart of our union. In the years since Oscar's passing, I have been excavating our marriage and pondering it. The writing of this book has been a soulful examination, a symbolic unearthing of certain memories and stories that Mercado might understand as a labor necessary to capture the fullness of a history, the ephemera and evidence of, in this case, a love story.

"Write the vision..."

—HABAKKUK 2:2, KJV

Turn away no more:
Why wilt thou turn away
The starry floor
The watry shore
Is giv'n thee till the break of day.

—WILLIAM BLAKE

Prelude

Once, while my husband and I were spending several months in Italy doing research at the American Academy in Rome, I found an intriguing book about marriage that someone had left behind in a communal sitting room. It was written by an American clergyman and, basically, held his testimony about how he had come to understand which of the many engaged couples whom he had counseled over the years would have an enduring marriage and which couples wouldn't. He admitted that when he first began officiating weddings, he was wrong most of the time about his predictions.

His final and correct realization, based on thoughtful observation over many years, was that an enduring union had not so much to do with the sharing of values (however helpful), hobbies, or temperaments. Instead, he came to understand that long-lasting wedlock was about two individuals having the same vision of their life together and an iron-clad commitment to that vision, one that would never be dulled by disappointment, perceived betrayal, hardship, or misfortune. The imperative was keeping that vision.

Oscar and I came warily to marriage for different reasons. He had suffered a very short-lived, dismal marital experience in his twenties that came to a nasty end. Then there was his nagging belief that he would die in his early forties, owing to the unanimous prediction of the physicians who had treated him when he nearly died of childhood nephritis. As for me? Well, I had come of age at a time when feminism had done its best to knock down traditional ideas about womanhood, fulfillment, and the notion that female happiness was connected to being a wife and mother.

Neither of us was *against* getting married, per se, but initially both of us held the belief that it wasn't terribly important. That we could have a wonderful and meaningful life together without the formal act of putting our lives on the page. And for eight years that is precisely how we managed our relationship. But that was the issue. I eventually understood, as did he, that a truly life-enhancing and profound union might need something more than management. For us, at that stage in our lives, it needed to be sanctioned and—in our case because of our belief in God—sanctified. It needed the imprimatur that comes from law. The idea of a legal seal associated with couplehood—even if dismissed by the most sophisticated and intellectual among us—is, after all, a fundament of civilization and society all the way back to the Old Testament. So, why not make it official?

Getting married changed the way we saw our life together and it changed us too. It made our "vision" of being a couple something to cherish and not underestimate. Marriage transformed our life; it gilded our bond.

A Library in a Church

I AM WORKING IN A SACRED PLACE. I am sitting at a desk in the library of an old, beloved cathedral as I write these words and begin the story of my marriage to the love of my life, Oscar Hijuelos. It is my first week writing here, and I take in the details with profound appreciation.

The colors on the walls, floor, and furniture surrounding me are earthy and calming. Crimson, moss, and sienna. Lining the walls are sturdy, black-painted bookshelves bearing placards with simple appellations such as *Fiction*, *Inspirational & Devotional*, *Parenting & Personal Growth*, *Children's Literature*, *Bible Stories*, and *Martin Luther & The Reformation*. It is an uncommonly well-stocked repository for a small-town ecclesiastical reading room and surprisingly au courant in its holdings of excellent fiction and nonfiction.

It is a very special gift to write in this benevolent, brick and stone church, by the name of First Lutheran—or

First Church, as it is affectionately called by the congregation—which sits upon a grassy hilltop overlooking the small city of Jamestown, New York, my birthplace. My mother is a member of First Lutheran, and I am spending time with her for a while. But I need a quiet space in which to write, away from the bustle of her house. To help me out, the pastor, Mark Swanson, the librarian, Wendy Larson, and the church council have graciously given me this library room in which to work.

Down the hall from my office is a blue stained glass-windowed chapel—a modern and tranquil space somewhat at odds with the original nineteenth-century architecture of the main part of the church—where I can go to pray and meditate. I hear Brian Bogey, esteemed Jamestown citizen and masterful musician, playing the organ in the nave above. His virtuoso playing thrills me. It settles me too. I detect uncommon ability and devotion in the way his fingers work the keyboard. And even when I can't see him, I know he's smiling in the way he always smiles during the 11:00 AM service each Sunday. There is a comforting sense of peace and safety in these rooms and passages of lemon-scented cleanliness. The sexton, Mike Key, has an office across from mine, and he labors constantly to keep the building immaculate. He moves silently, I notice, and is consistently attentive to me. Every time I enter the church, I feel his respect.

To say that I feel honored to be in this edifice to think about my late husband, examine our life together, and configure a narrative that conveys the sense of spirit and mystery of our life together is an understatement. The act of writing a memoir in this building has the sacramental about it.

But there is a problem: I don't know how to explain the essence of our writing marriage. It seems an impossibility. Even though I feel the necessity to do so—to elaborate on its form and content—this is an exigency I don't understand. I am following an inner voice. I am an acolyte to this mandate: to know that our marriage happened, to recall and memorialize it. Yet this is not enough.

I will try to give our history a niche in time. I will try to make our story sing. It seems that the definition of my life depends on it.

A Brief Interlude

BEFORE MY STORY BEGINS, I need to set the stage by revealing a few details about our origins.

In the 1980s, at the time of Oscar's arrival on the American cultural platform, it was virtually unheard of for a child of poor Latino immigrants to make his mark on the US literary turf of Philip Roth, Saul Bellow, William Styron, John Updike, and John Cheever, among others. He was the first Latino to win a Pulitzer Prize for Fiction. This is often said of Oscar, as a kind of advertisement or commercial byline. But it really means something quite monumental. I believe my husband's unlikely path leading to literary achievement, as related in his memoir *Thoughts Without Cigarettes*, is necessary to note in order to fully appreciate the constitution of our writing marriage. Why?

Oscar broke boundaries by way of extraordinary drive, spirit, and individual reliance. And he achieved being a "first" in American literary history despite the flow of aggressive negativity in the staid enclave that determined what was remarkable in American letters.*

Strength of enormous will and an appreciation of his Spanish constitution via Cuban pizazz. This is what Oscar was made of and used to push forward, out of an environment of going nowhere. With almost no encouragement or prompting from his immediate circle, including his family, he made the leap to a life of opportunity. His aspirational character and imagination propelled him. Once he started City College in New York City, he found mentors—such as novelists Donald Barthelme and Frederic Tuten—who became not only his professors, but true friends and colleagues, just as the figure of Dr. Aloysius Hunt is for Mercado in *Blue Antiquity*. Here is an accounting of Oscar's quest for betterment through education, fictional in presentation but totally nonfictional in truth, from the novel:

> So naturally, he wanted out, and what better way was there than to read books, and to get himself all educated, though it was never easy. His high school had been rough, its classrooms and hallways so congested and noisy as to make it hard for anyone to

* To this day, there is a critical current that works against the strain of the American voice coming from Spanish/Hispanic culture. This bias is hundreds of years old and crosses continents. It is related to a rooted academic, political, and cultural/philosophical standing that claims superiority, which is too lengthy to address here, but is real. And it is associated with the invention of the printing press at a time when Protestant dominion was gradually gaining steam on the global stage after centuries of Spanish Catholic rule. This Protestant gain was finally established in the late sixteenth century with the defeat of the Spanish Armada by England.

think, let alone feel special and "upwardly bound." Putting the gangs, the drugs, the stairwell rapes, the stabbings and the daily hassles of just being there aside, Mercado could never study much at home, his mind vexed by the inertia he felt around him. To put it bluntly, no matter how bright he sometimes felt himself to be, some dragging down of his confidence still wrapped itself around his every aspiration.

Nevertheless, he made it through high school and onwards to college, first in the Bronx at a two-year school, then to City College as a history major, and in his later incarnation, while a substitute teacher in the New York City public school system, taking courses towards a master's degree at night. It was there, in Harlem, in a classroom in an old stone building, after the template of Yale, whose foundations had gone up over a nun's graveyard, that Mercado, then in his late twenties and attending a course in ancient history, first met Doctor Aloysius Hunt.

And I? Well, as the daughter of second-generation Americans—living comfortably in a lovely house in a beautiful neighborhood with all kinds of advantages that often accompany American middle-class life—I had an understanding, by virtue of my Lutheran formation and my interpretation of biblical verse to understand how much my soul would complement his, even though it might not have been obvious to those around us. We were meant to be.

Spanish

WITHOUT QUESTION, other than our mutual love of literature, Spanish was fundamental to our relationship and marriage. It was Spanish—that sensual, mellifluous language—that explained a lot about our unity through thick and thin. So important was the fact that I was bilingual and intimately knew the Iberian-Hispanic cultures to which the language belonged, as well as my formal collegiate education conducted in the language, that I doubt Oscar would have made the switch from partner to spouse otherwise.

As for me, well...I might have considered dating someone who didn't speak Spanish, but I would never have married a man who did not speak it. And Oscar, I know, would not have tied the knot with a woman who did not have a clue, as he expressed to me, about *cubanía*. He needed to marry someone who could fully understand his Cuban background and relate her thoughts in *castellano*. Period. This is how important agency in Spanish was to both of us. This romance language had multiple layers of symbolic meaning that English did not hold for either of us. For Oscar it involved pride of origin and familial dignity; for me it involved intellectual growth.

I suppose there was an element of secrecy about our bond in castellano too, something that cemented our mutual attraction. This feature of our relationship was mostly unknown to the world and especially to the New York literary scene. The latter operated on an English-only stage at the time. Few seemed to understand that our foundation was in the Latino element of our society, and this was reflected in our private life, our friendships, our cuisine at home, and our appreciation of Spanish art and literature and the motherland herself, Spain.

How this came to be is rather complex and unusual, I suppose, given that when I began to study Spanish, as a child of ten in my remote little town, the language was not considered a popular or necessary subject of instruction in public schools. New York State, in the years in which I was a youngster, was unique in our country. There was a massive influx of Puerto Ricans—Americans by birth—in the 1950s and '60s to New York City. Educators viewed this migration as an opportunity to add the language and Puerto Rican cultural awareness to formal curriculum. It was thought of as a fun and interesting opportunity to learn about Hispanic culture in communities like Jamestown. (Any serious ESL interest was relegated to Manhattan public schools.)

I was one of a small group of children chosen by my fourth-grade teacher to take Spanish lessons a few times a week in the library of Milton J. Fletcher Elementary School. I loved it. I remember practicing a few words out loud on my short walk home after class ended each day. Smiling all the way. I was chosen to be one of these lucky few because it was determined that I had a good ear and was a very engaged pupil. I was an early reader; I won lots of prizes for reading the most chapbooks each month. And I was enamored with music. I liked piano, violin, and anything that emitted beautiful notes. I also loved to sing.

In junior high school, I realized—no, I *understood*—that the Spanish language would be a major part of my life. (This was owing to a psychic awareness that I explain more fully elsewhere in these pages.) I did not understand just how Spanish would affect my life, but I knew that it would be essential to my future, along with music.

In college, I excelled in my studies. With the support and encouragement of my professors, who reinforced my certainty that I would claim a very particular future that involved speaking Spanish, I decided to enter a doctoral program in Iberian-Hispanic Literature at Indiana University. I chose Indiana over other great schools because—at the time—the department was one of the best and largest in the country. It boasted a superb faculty with some of the finest scholars of Spanish and Latin American literature in the world. It was big, really vibrant, with many tenured faculty. This was important to me.

I left the department, however, after I received my MA because I knew that my path was meant to be different from the ordinary approach to scholarship. I realized that I was being directed. (That feeling of "understanding" was insistent and not to be ignored.) Off to New York City I went, without knowing a soul there, with excitement to begin a career in editing, writing about, and translating Latin American literature. (An almost unheard-of professional direction; hence my need to create it.) And, indeed, my career took off in the world of Spanish and Latin American literature just as I had predicted. Quickly.

Oscar's dance with Spanish was completely different from my own, of course. There was no formal education. Born into a Spanish-speaking household, he spoke as a native before he fell grievously ill with nephritis at the age of four. This was the wound that would affect Oscar's understanding of his life forever. A linguistic sword came down on Oscar's psyche; his yearlong hospitalization in an English-only environment isolated him from his family and, thus, his natural confidence in Spanish. It would divide his life into before and after. English would take center stage at this point in his development and would change the way Oscar thought about communication forever.

Oscar was often quoted by journalists and others in the public arena as saying that he "lost" his Spanish after nearly dying from nephritis. But I would like to lend some perspective to his thinking about *what* he lost. My understanding of Oscar's "loss" was different from his own on the matter.

There is no denying—none, on my part—that if I had not been completely fluent in Spanish, I would not have had as much influence on Oscar as I had, both in our romantic relationship as well as in Oscar's professional life. The fact that he could depend on me for everything—from the correct pronunciation of a Spanish word that was unfamiliar to him to choosing the perfect vacation spot for total relaxation in Mallorca to inviting my opinion of a novel by, let's say, Mexican Juan Rulfo or Chilean novelist Pepe Donoso, to feeling comfortable in a social setting where Spanish was the only language spoken—cannot be refuted. I was his *solid* in these regards. He could confidently rely on me, and he did.

But there is something more to all of this. The truth is that Oscar never lost his ability to speak Spanish; he lost his confidence in *being* and *living* in it.

When Oscar and I first started dating, my entire social scene revolved around friends who were native Spanish speakers (also fluent in English), and this situation both attracted and scared him. He loved that I was so immersed in and familiar with the culture, but he also found it somewhat daunting. He knew that Spanish would be expected of him, especially with his newfound status of famous Latino writer. Oscar, truth be told, would hardly ever resort to a word in his native tongue at those gatherings, preferring to carry on in English. Believe me, he could have held his own...if only he had understood his capability. But there was always a psychological impediment: the trauma of the childhood hospitalization and the fear of speaking Spanish because of it. He simply did not have the confidence to assert himself in his family's native tongue. Public life, for him, required English.

There is a brief allusion to this personal and vexing linguistic duality in *Blue Antiquity* when the protagonist, Mercado, is trying to communicate in Italian with a stranger he has just met in a little Roman restaurant. Oscar certainly, in my view, inhabits Mercado's thinking in the following:

> "Please," he remembered the portly man saying, "just in English, huh? I prefer it to the way you speak Italian."
>
> A little stung, for Mercado got quite well along in Rome with the language, he nevertheless withdrew behind a veil of good-natured modesty, the same way he did growing up when he'd encounter so many of the Cubans and Puerto Ricans of his family's acquaintances, some of whom—but not all—were somewhat judgmental of his New York–bred Spanish; that is to say, the Spanish of a wayward kid trying to get along in the outside world, whose preference for years had been to speak English, but one of a street borne hybrid, speckled like a dirty mirror with "ain't"s, "you know," and "hey, man"s, not to mention all the curse words that flew like crows through his head and had to be cleared out of there, educationally speaking, with a later-in-life industrial strength vacuum cleaner, that, indeed, gave him an aloof air. And so, he supposed, there were Italians every bit as snobby as some Latinos, or Hispanics as they were called in those days, were about their Spanish. Or as Mercado sometimes (still) thought, there would always be someone around to draw the line between Mercado and his Latino-ness.

The truth is this: After Oscar returned home from the Connecticut hospital in which he had been recovering, he listened to his parents and his brother, José, speak in *castellano*. Oscar told his interviewers that when his parents would include him in these Spanish-speaking conversations, he would speak in English only. But I doubt this is accurate. Why? Because when he was alone with me, and completely relaxed, he could carry on a conversation in fluid Spanish. (He also dreamt in Spanish. How many times I was awoken by Oscar speaking aloud in perfect grammatical sentences and the precise Cuban vowel/consonant spin of the vernacular I can't even begin to count.) How could he speak the language so well if he had never taken a formal class in it? Or perhaps better put: How could Oscar know Spanish in a native way if he had not been totally immersed in it as a child?

After Oscar died, a very dear, old elementary school chum of his, Victor Cruz, was reminiscing with me about Oscar's youth. He revealed this fact: Oscar was speaking Spanish to him when they were both around ten years old. He knew this because he himself was the child of Cuban immigrants, new to New York City at that age, and couldn't speak a word of English. Who was the only child in the classroom at Corpus Christi Elementary School who befriended him by chatting away in Spanish? Oscar.

The linguistic tug of war that existed in my husband was one that he himself created, I surmise, to explain the sense of psychic loneliness—and grief—he lived with all his life. It is my view that even though Oscar was an American through and through, he inherited the pain of displacement that his Cuban-born parents carried with them in their souls: the melancholia of immigration. Even if immigration is chosen or desired, leaving the homeland is just plain hard. There is so much struggle along with potential gain. And, for Oscar, a kind of gloom could take hold of him because of it.

Regardless of Oscar's feelings about his proficiency in Spanish, it is undeniable that the language—spoken and written—influenced his writing. The Romance language of his parents imposed its will on the hybrid lingua franca of his birthplace. Any Spanish-speaking person who reads Oscar's fiction in English will immediately see the familiar poetry and heart in it, the rhythms and cadences of Spanish mischievously playing all over the succinct and precise Germanic undertones of his English syntax. His ear leaned toward the Romance element, stressing it, rather than bending to the more clipped and cogent counterpart. The focus on intricate description, the lean toward *verso* and lengthy elaboration with flourish and sweep are hallmarks of his writing style, along with his preoccupation of soul, of which this brief excerpt is an example:

> In Corsica, in a place called Filotosa, he had picnicked in an ancient garden of Eden, and thought of it a "land of sleep" for everywhere he looked, there were olive trees and dainty nets spread below on the ground, on which peasants dozed beneath the tranquil sun. In the south of France, along the coast near Marseille, he had watched the moon rising over the black crescent of the horizon and waited for something to rise out

of the stirring dark waters; and in those moments he understood why the ancient people had believed in Neptune.

Oscar dove into the bleakness of our human condition to surface with light. Literary chiaroscuro was his method. This is what Oscar took of Iberian-Hispanic culture and brought to the literature of the USA.

Imagery and Influence

I BELIEVE A KIND OF INDESCRIBABLE, protective veil hung over my life with Oscar. I didn't fully realize this until recently, when I was ruminating on the importance of various religious traditions' teachings, imagery, and symbols in our marriage. For me, the sources of my spiritual strength and identity have come overwhelmingly from my Lutheran formation, which puts emphasis on biblical stories from both Old and New Testaments, liturgical affirmations in the weekly Sunday service, and the scholarship of Lutheran giants such as Martin Luther and, much later, Dietrich Bonhoeffer.

But Oscar was different. He was searching for spiritual lessons from many sources. He was fascinated by all kinds of religious histories, even though he drew sustenance and found a certain "tree of life" power from most notably Buddhism along with Catholicism. In fact, two visits to the Himalayas were life-changing for my husband: The first was to Bhutan and Nepal in 1993 and the second was to Nepal and Tibet in 1998. Both were trekking expeditions and very much, for Oscar, metaphysical odysseys. Each sojourn, especially the first, had profound mystical implications for him that truly changed the way he understood God and love.

Because Oscar became so interested in Buddhism, I too was made more familiar with this faith. Among our various circles of friends was one that was partial to Buddhist teachings and practice. We both found our friends in this community to be exceptionally serene and comforting. Friends such as Helen Tworkov, founder of *Tricycle: The Buddhist Review*, and the eminent psychiatrist and author Mark Epstein. Occasionally, Lou Reed and Laurie Anderson were companions at certain Buddhist-oriented events, too.

I am reluctant to share specifics about two incidents, during the first trip to that matchless region of soaring mountains and ethereal grandeur, that Oscar related to me, because he asked that I not recount them, ever, to anyone. They were nothing short of mind-boggling, supernatural, and contradictory to imagery we know of as Christian. I will, however, allow myself to describe just one of Oscar's encounters with Buddhist energies on his first trip to the region. It happened that Oscar came face-to-face with an otherworldly being in Nepal—not animal, not human—that floated in the air before him, as if a guide, on a formidable mountain range. He drew a picture of this creature in a diary that he kept of that journey. The ethereal being had a head, eyes, and a tail-like body. It was a "comforting and companionable spirit," he explained to me, and it bestowed upon Oscar a sense of peace, safety, and well-being. It beckoned him to move forward on his trek with confidence and total peace. And Oscar did just that.

Oscar was inclined to understand reality on a psychic level, as is true of me, which can be a bit jarring, maybe even strange, for some. He had what is commonly known as a sixth sense for sure, even letting me know repeatedly and in a matter-of-fact tone during our marriage that he knew how he would die (although he never told me the particulars as he understood that it would certainly destroy me with dread).

But getting back to Oscar's two important treks to the mystical lands of the Himalayas, I can say with certainty that he came to a decision about marrying me on the second sojourn in 1998. Before he left, I had not known that this trip was meant to serve as a "meditative time-out" to understand several issues facing him, one of which was to help him see his future with me clearly. The night of his return from Kathmandu in the late summer of that year, he proposed like this, "Let's do that thing with the bishop."

A Writing Marriage

SO, WHAT IS A WRITING MARRIAGE? When I first thought of this description of my life with Oscar, I didn't think so much of the meaning as I did the musicality of the title. But I knew instinctively that our relationship was founded on something profound and deep that rooted us to literary art, a quest to illuminate the hidden elements of reality, true love, and respect, and the mysterious power of words to create, remake, and heal. Literature, for Oscar, was the highest art form (although music was a close second) because, simply, as he would say, "We remember how humanity has lived and thought through words written down for the ages."

Our marriage formally began with our wedding vows, which were rewritten by Oscar when Dr. James Forbes, who officiated at our nuptials, gave us a boilerplate that my interdenominational church, The Riverside Church in New York City, used as a standard. A brief digression about our pre-wedding interview with Dr. Forbes. It was an encounter that I will never forget. It was a meeting that was special, or let's say blessed.

Oscar, knowing how important my church was to me, deferred to the authority of Riverside's conventions and traditions regarding our marriage. He was perfectly fine having the wedding ceremony in my Protestant church, although we both wanted to have a Catholic priest participate to honor Oscar's religious upbringing. This was not to be, as the clergyman of his parish church was unavailable.

The first step was meeting with the senior pastor to find out if he was comfortable officiating at our wedding. So Oscar and I went one afternoon to meet him in his office.

Dr. Forbes could not have been more congenial, and was very encouraging about having a Catholic priest co-officiate. His mellow presence put us at ease. In a kindly way, he asked us questions about our relationship. He wanted to know what we believed about marriage and our expectations about being husband and wife.

Oscar was wearing a bright orange corduroy shirt that day. And at one point in our conversation, he said to Dr. Forbes, "I honestly didn't believe that I would ever get married again. It's really something I had written off a long time ago after my short-lived, first marriage." Oscar's face had turned the exact same color as his shirt. He was nervous.

Dr. Forbes, seeing Oscar's vulnerability, had the perfect reply in his soothing, oboe-toned register, "Well, Oscar, consider it a true blessing from God above."

Those words acted as a benediction for us as we happily walked out of the pastoral offices toward our future.

But before leaving, Dr. Forbes had asked us if we wanted to make any changes to the vows that he had given us to peruse. We did. I left the editing to Oscar, and by the time he had read and rewritten almost every line, the original was so redacted that you could hardly see the type. Oscar's distinctive, loopy handwriting was sprawling and created a kind of crochet of two entirely different threads of statements. I remember when he handed me his version of what he thought we should say to one another, I smiled and nodded. His eyes were twinkling.

We recited these words to one another with such honesty and reverence the evening of our Christmas time wedding that it seemed as if they were not vows but an antiphonal prayer. There was not an ironic or formal note in our offering—just us being us. Loving the words, loving the articulation of our truth, and loving the fact that we were getting married by literature. This was our commitment to one another. Oscar's rhythms and the style of his writing were evident in the first act of our new life together.

I remember with exact detail the morning following our ethereal evening celebration on December 12, 1998. I found Oscar in a chair in his snuggery, at the back of our apartment. He was weeping. "What's wrong?" I asked as I went to hug him. He looked up and said, "Our wedding was so beautiful, Lori. It was just so beautiful."

A few days later I noticed that he had arranged dozens of cobalt blue glass votive candles—the ones that lit our wedding dinner in the cathedral's marbled hall with a painted midnight blue ceiling of stars—within the bookshelves of our dining room. We had bought these votives on a whim one wintry afternoon, upon entering a midtown Manhattan monastery attached to a Catholic chapel that Oscar particularly liked.

Tears are streaming down my cheeks as I write of these recollections. Such was the tenderness and sweetness of my husband.

Yet this is just the beginning of what would become a writing marriage. The fullness of our commitment would develop over the fifteen years of our formal union. It was not always smooth sailing. Whenever my husband was in the thick of writing, it was uneasy in our household. Sometimes there were tears and moments of thunder. Oscar was a man of highly descriptive commentary, and he could explode with withering verbosity if he was under too much stress. Such outbursts were unsettling. On the occasions when this would happen, I was usually silent in response. I knew that to answer would only make things worse. But, true to his gentlemanly core, these moments were quickly followed by very witty apologies in writing, roses, and kisses.

The love was always there. Always. But, as in any human relationship, there were forces that came at us, unexpected strains and influences that had to be addressed and handled. In our case, the difficulties resulted from the publishing environment and the weighty literary society of New York City and the pressures of it, not to mention Oscar's international fame (the kind that distorts priorities and enlivens inconsequential fissures) and all the opportunities and attractions that come with the notion of *importance*. But I knew, as did Oscar, that no matter what...we would always be together.

It was the purpose of writing in our lives—the act of creating separate, very different bodies of work—that always put us back on track any time we were a little shaky. We simply loved, admired, and honored each other's creative leanings. And we were attracted to each other powerfully.

I think the most memorable example of Oscar's intense love for me in this regard, his attention to the creative dimension of my being, occurred a few months before he died. I remember the details as if they had just happened. It was summertime. We were in our Connecticut redoubt on Long Island Sound, and I had just received bound galleys of my third novel, *A Stitch in Air*, from the publisher, Texas Tech University Press. Immediately, Oscar asked to have a copy so he could read it at once. As soon as I handed him the novel, he rushed to his studio. I knew that he would have a pen in hand to comment and/or make edits as he made his way through it, page by page, with his exacting eye. And, so, I was a bit nervous. I wondered what he would think of my book about sixteenth-century Spanish nuns now that he had the complete story in front of him, instead of just sections that he had been reading as I wove the narrative together over the previous years.

I took a copy from the stack and started reading my novel too. I wanted to make sure that I corrected any typos or incorrect information before the copy went to press for the final printing.

A few hours later, I heard Oscar rushing up the stairs that led to our cozy home. At the top of the landing, I heard him call out, "Lori!" I left the living room and just as I entered the entry, Oscar exclaimed, "This is a very good thing you have done, a very good thing, a very good thing!" He was beaming. I had rarely seen him so joyful. I knew that his comment was aimed at not only what he thought was the literary quality of my writing, but the intent of my book...to shed light on the little understood dynamics of conventual life in the 1500s. And the fact that not all nuns living in the cloister wanted to be confined to such a restrictive and cramped lifestyle. Often fathers and elder brothers forced their daughters and sisters into this arrangement with strenuous objection from the women who were about to be cloistered forever.

Oscar was, at heart, a feminist. He believed in the power of women and celebrated their achievement and success in whatever form that word implied. He truly admired the female sex and thought very highly of women who cherished and sought independence and made their mark in history. (For what it's worth, he esteemed Hillary Clinton.)

"You like it?" I asked.

"Like it?" he responded. "I love it. I am so proud of you, Lori. I am so proud of you."

He stood there, with my book in hand, and continued to smile at me. Then he hugged and kissed me. "I'm going back to the studio to read it again." He grinned in that old familiar sweet way of his, impossible to describe other than to say it could melt the stoniest of hearts.

"This is a very good thing you have done. A very good thing," he repeated as he made his way slowly down the stairs.

If ever there were a happier me, I couldn't remember.

Well, maybe there is. It involves another episode of our life at Killam's Point, a nearly invisible one...were it not for the fact that I loved to lounge in my sitting room, high above the bay in front of our Connecticut home... and watch whatever was happening on our private little beach.

One morning, after Oscar had descended the staircase to go to his studio, I was sipping my third cup of coffee and looking at the high tide along the shore below me. Suddenly, Oscar appeared on the sand with a very long pole of some kind. After peering at him for a while, I realized he was holding a lengthy tree branch. It was whitewashed from the sea. A beautiful, natural pole as it were.

But what was he doing there, standing on the edge of the beach with this long branch? I was puzzled.

I watched, day after day, as Oscar went to the beach at high tide and stood looking at the Long Island Sound with that driftwood branch.

And then, one afternoon I went down to his studio to ask him a question about dinner plans, and I saw a familiar beach towel hanging on the terrace rail. It was from Walmart—just a simple large but comfy towel that I had bought on a whim one day when I was shopping and that he had loved. He lost it at sea one afternoon after someone had accidentally pushed it off the dock.

"Oscar," I asked, "is that the towel that you lost, drying out on the terrace?"

"Yes, Pupsie," he answered with a huge grin. "I found it. I love that towel."

"Why is it so important?" I asked.

"Because you gave it to me, Pupsie bear."

Books

Books were at the heart of Oscar's and my meeting, romance, and marriage. Our reading and writing of books, and our pleasure and delight in them, shaped the way we envisioned our life together. Words were our foundation. Perhaps the most accurate way to describe how Oscar felt about books is a fictional musing by Mark Twain in Oscar's posthumously published novel, *Twain & Stanley Enter Paradise*: "Books, I then concluded, are my water, my evening and morning meal, my sunlight and garden, and what words spill from my pencil are my gestures of thanks for that fact." They were the most cherished possession in our home and the most pleasing element of our apartment's décor. Everywhere we looked, a pile of books greeted us. My husband lauded the importance of written erudition and its transformative power in every single novel he wrote.

Oscar and I met at a reception for a famous Latin American novelist at the organization where I began my career just out of graduate school. The organization is now known as the Americas Society but back in 1981, when we first laid eyes on each other, it went by The Center for Inter-American Relations. It was a posh establishment, created by David Rockefeller, for mainly well-heeled members and guests who shared a common interest in all things South American, Caribbean, and Mexican. CEOs of major US corporations and various American and Latin American diplomats and lawyers were numerous among them. But it also became a cozy gathering place for striving Latino artists who had discovered its importance in the publishing world. They knew that the institution championed and appreciated the Spanish language and the cultures associated with it. They knew, too, that the Center advocated for their books' publication at houses such as Knopf, FSG, and Pantheon. Artists and writers of Latin American heritage who were living in New York City loved this fact. And they loved the camaraderie they found there, as it was lacking in a very large way in Manhattan, not to mention the country at large. In short, it was a very special, singular place. An establishment of elegant diplomacy.

At the time, Oscar was completing his first novel and the evening we were introduced to each other by a generous, mutual friend, Guatemalan-born David Unger, was one he had planned on working on his manuscript. (He wrote at night, after a full day's labor at an advertising agency in midtown.) Instead, Oscar was cajoled into accompanying David to make a stop at 680 Park Avenue to join the festivities on the second floor of the mansion before starting a long evening's toil. David wanted Oscar to meet me, and he knew that I would be flitting about the elegant Salon Simón Bolívar as hostess, introducing the attendees and encouraging amiable small talk about writing, publishing, and Latin American literature.

I can't say that I remember much about that first encounter, but I do recall that Oscar was quiet and shy. Intense too. He had an aura that was potent. His small, hazel eyes were laser bright and mischievous. I intuited that there was nothing moderate about him. He inhabited a vitality that was so palpable that I felt it, literally, charge into me. A few words were exchanged off-handedly, with David initiating the conversation.

"Lori, this is Oscar Hijuelos, a Cuban force in the community. He is working on a novel. In fact, he would be home right now if I hadn't convinced him to come here to meet you."

I smiled at Oscar. "So nice to meet you, Oscar," I responded cheerily. "How wonderful that you are working on your first book. I would love to read it when you are ready to share some pages."

Oscar stared at my eyes, my neck, my legs. A slow up and down. "Sure," he responded as the light in his eyes suddenly burned brighter.

* * *

Over the next several years we circled one another. I say "circled" because we seemed to eye each other without truly engaging at the receptions and readings he continued to attend at The Center. I was preoccupied with adjusting to New York City life after a sheltered midwestern and Upstate New York formation before landing in the metropolis. I was a little wary.

I was having, I guess you could say, an Alice in Wonderland initiation in Manhattan. If I wasn't negotiating a particularly tricky romance, I was searching for an apartment that I could afford, which was always consuming my thoughts after the workday. I might have been hosting a lot of fancy nighttime receptions, but I was not living it up. I was focused on surviving.

In 1983 an event I had not expected would put me on a very concrete course that would change my life forever.

The novel that Oscar had been composing when I first met him had been published by Persea Books, a small house run by Michael and Karen Braziller, that was dedicated to releasing very fine literary works. *Our House in the Last World*, Oscar's first published novel, had become something of a hit, at least for people in the know. Literary agents, industry pundits, reviewers for major newspapers, critics, and highfalutin honorary societies had taken note of Oscar's beautiful writing.

One day my supervisor, Rosario Santos, came to me with a copy of the novel and said, "Why don't you read this and tell me what you think? Oscar gave it to me at the fair over at the Armory. He is so nice. Such a sweet young man."

I took the novel home with me that night and read it, first page to last, in bed. I remember that I could not stop crying as I read page after page. The sorrow and grief, the hardships and constant misses in life were so visceral and so real that I was experiencing—for the very first time—a sense of true disadvantage and material poverty in America. (This was an America I did not know personally at all.) Oscar's writing had taken me to a place that I had only read about in newspapers and essays: a place of want and despair. And yet...*Our House* was infused with luminosity. The hope was in his pen. He had made the daring choice to expose the painful truth of his own family's place in society, what he called "second-classness." (*Empress of the Splendid Season*, more than any other of his novels, I believe, brilliantly reflects exactly what this societal condition felt like growing up in West Harlem in the 1960s and '70s.) When I came to the last page, I knew I had to present Oscar as the luminary I understood him to be to our distinguished Center membership.

The next morning, I told Rosario that Oscar was "the real thing." I excitedly asked her, "Can I interview him for my program, Books and Breakfast? I know that he is not technically Latin American (ours was a literary office devoted to promoting writers from South America, Mexico, and the Caribbean), but I know our audience will be interested in this book. Oscar is the son of Cuban immigrants, and this narrative showcases the plight of the Spanish-speaking community in the US. It is wonderful. And timely. The writing is amazing."

Rosario looked at me and smiled. She was won over by my enthusiasm, I could see.

The Center's third-floor conference room was full on the morning of Oscar's Q & A. The guests included Jeffrey Hoffeld, a dapper art dealer and one of Oscar's closest friends, and the cute, bubbly woman Oscar was dating, Leslie. The event went extremely well, Oscar all smiles and often embarrassed by my compliments and sometimes cheeky inquiries. We were a bit flirtatious, but our playful banter was in fun. After all, he had a girlfriend. And I was dating someone.

"Oscar," I asked, "how much of you is in the character of Hector, especially when you describe his childhood years? It seems as if you are painting a portrait of yourself in that little, towheaded boy."

Oscar blushed crimson before answering, "Miss Carlson! Do I really have to answer that?" He laughed.

"Alright. You can pass. Next question." I looked at the audience and winked. "The novel ends with a dreamlike sequence involving allusions to a fairy tale and ancient airs and dances, as it were," I commented. "Why end this fiercely realistic story about the Santinio family with such a fantastical flourish?"

This was more to his liking, and he ran with it. In the process, he was revealing to me that he was an intellectual. He wove a fascinating account of method and artistry and his broad knowledge of literature. His comments ended on a personal note. "Actually," he mused, "my titles come to me in dreams. In the case of *Our House in the Last World,* I dreamt that I saw the title on the spine of a book on a library shelf."

I touched his arm as I thanked him for such a candid and enjoyable conversation, and we concluded our conversation to applause.

* * *

Unexpectedly, Oscar appeared at the Center a few days later. Marion, our perky, upbeat receptionist, rang me to say that I had a visitor. And did I have time to see Mr. Hijuelos?

A few minutes later there was elegant and shy Oscar at my door, dressed very nicely with silk cravat, holding a large, exuberant bouquet of red roses.

This little hint of a romantic direction in our friendship, however, would not develop fully until six years later. From 1983 to 1989 there was simmering intrigue. I remember that if he broke a lunch date, always five minutes before the appointed hour, with an apologetic, "Lori, I'm sorry but I just can't stop writing now. Is it okay?"—there was laughter on my part. "No problem." And then, the next morning when I arrived at my office, a red rose would be waiting for me at the reception desk.

In June 1989, when both of our personal and professional circumstances had changed, the timing was right for passion and the love between us that I now know was divine design.

Divergent Backgrounds

THE FACT THAT OSCAR AND I ever met is somewhat of a miracle, given our sharply different backgrounds, birthplaces, and upbringings, but the similarities in our natures, values, and interests were encouraged and fostered by these very same contradictory beginnings. In the twelve years since my late husband passed away, I have done a lot of ruminating about God's providence in our finding each other and ultimately marrying. Our meeting happened in New York City, yes, where we both happily lived, but the push and force of that beautiful and wondrous encounter began in our childhoods in two dissimilar settings: Oscar's in the edgy, exposed neck of Harlem and mine in the remote, protective cocoon of Jamestown, New York. Jamestown, as a New York State locale, is about as far away from New York City as you can get, geographically and philosophically. However small and quaint, though, it can lay claim to being the birthplace of cultural giants, such as Lucille Ball, Roger Tory Peterson, Robert H. Jackson, Roger Goodell, and 10,000 Maniacs. It boasts lovely scenery and very visible traditions, particularly Swedish and Italian (the two cultures being those of my father and mother respectively). Jamestown is the epitome of an American small town. Ask a stranger on the street to identify the three most important things in life and you'll have a sense of what 99 percent of middle America believes.

When I was growing up in the late 1970s, most of the youth in Jamestown was wholesome. But I was even more protected "from stuff" than most of the teens in my high school. In my free time I liked to stay home and read, think, and play the piano. I enjoyed the company of my parents and wanted to spend time with them. I did not go out. No partying at all. I was a dreamer. Dreaming and reading in my chair in the living room. My passions: literature, philosophy, the Spanish language, and music. I was naive and extremely protected, yet strong-willed and motivated. I stumped a lot of people. On the outside I was petite, delicate, proper, and reserved, but I had invisible convictions, inclinations, and intellectual proclivities that were fierce and focused. I was a cerebral innocent. Or as one of my professors later in life would say: "An iron dove."

I was also very involved with my Lutheran church. I sang with a youth choir called the Kirk Singers, and volunteered often to help elderly and infirm members of the congregation. I was deeply committed to my faith and, for lack of a better word, a bit of a mystic. To this day, my prescience is something that both troubles and cushions me, depending on the circumstances. For instance, I know when a family member is sick or ailing even if I am thousands of miles away. I can sense a death on the other side of the globe. (When my adorable, teenage cousin died tragically in a drowning accident on Chautauqua Lake, I woke up with a start, trembling, while I was staying in the tiny Austrian village of Rastenfeld.) On a different note, I can predict when someone is going to call to share good news. Among the brighter of these kinds of transcendental moments relates to the day that Oscar was called by his publisher, Roger Straus, to convey that he had won the Pulitzer Prize. In the morning, about five hours before the announcement, I told Oscar it was going to happen. The circumstances were these: We were taking a break from his busy international book tour and were resting at an acquaintance's country house in upstate New York. It was Maundy Thursday 1990. The agenda for the day was to go antiquing in the town of Saugerties. After stopping for breakfast along the way, I asked Oscar when he thought the Pulitzers would be announced. "Why do you want to know that?" he asked somewhat harshly.

I answered, "Because you are going to win, Oscar."

Oscar was really upset with me. He yelled that I was being "presumptuous" because he couldn't believe that I would set him up for a downfall, a total heartbreak. "How could you say that?" he asked again and again. But at that time Oscar did not comprehend I had the ability to predict events that were going to happen with absolute certainty. I remember feeling terrible that I had verbalized what I knew in my heart because it had troubled him so much. It was then I decided I would never convey such understandings to him again.

I only surfaced from my gloom that day when, just as I predicted, Oscar's agent telephoned us while I was making lunch back at the house after our morning shopping spree. She told me that we could "not leave the house under any circumstances" because Oscar was going to get a call from Roger Straus imminently. "A very important call." I remember now the expressions on Oscar's face as he listened to the news that I had already shared with him earlier that morning: shock, gratitude, and elation. When he hung up the phone he went outside, looked up at the sky, and said, "If only my father were here to experience this with me."

And Oscar in his teens? Well, in his own words, he was a "dese and dose kid." A Cuban-American boy with a lot of heart who was clever, imaginative, resourceful, super bright (but hid it), sassy, witty, and combative if need be. Oscar played tough to his incredible sweetness. So, like my adolescent self, he was misunderstood...but in the reverse. People who knew him well saw that he was strong, tough, hip, and willing to take on anyone who got in his way. Quick of tongue. Feisty and naughty. He was typical of an urban-born teen in a poor neighborhood of diverse race and ethnicity in that he experimented and partied and hung out on the street. Underneath it all, though, he was an intellectual, extremely sensitive, artistic, spiritual, generous, and family-oriented. A dreamer whose great preoccupations were literature, music, art, and the Spanish language. He was seeking knowledge. And he was aiming for wisdom and achievement.

Two totally opposite environments nurtured in us the same fervent passions.

The first time my husband visited Jamestown was when he came to meet my parents in the early days of our courtship. As we drove from Buffalo Niagara International Airport to Jamestown, Oscar remarked on the acres of cow pasture, extensive farmland, vineyards, orchards, woods, and glens, marsh, and rolling hills for miles and miles, and the ponds, rivers, streams, and lakes everywhere. I am reminded of Mercado's appreciative eye as he takes in the beauty of the Italian countryside in this excerpt from *Blue Antiquity*:

> Oh, but the highlights of those months, interspersed in Mercado's head as he walked around the grounds: first came that daily immersion in the quietude of nature, for Mercado, out in the field, soon discovered that despite his urban orientation to the world, he absolutely loved the countryside's beauty—the pines and olive and fig trees, the fields of wild flowers, of violets and angelica, and the sight of sheep and horses roaming in the distance, of the dreamy miasma floating in the air, of wispy dragonflies and fritillaries drifting around, the perfumed wisteria cascading over lane walls, and of the most incredible bird song, sparrows darting, bouncing daintily on their narrow heels everywhere.

His opening comments as we drove through the city center toward the locale of my parents' house, were: "It's a ghost town. No one is here. Where are the people?"

He looked confused and disappointed. He continued to muse, "I don't understand why there aren't any people around."

The fact that there was no street life to speak of—the small city staging with few visible inhabitants, similar to every other American small town—failed to register with him as "normal." I explained that people were inside their houses or in the backyard or shopping somewhere in a mall. "But you don't see them," he repeated with not a little alarm. Thinking about how strange the scenery must have seemed to him, I hugged him and answered, "You're right. It's kind of lonely looking here, isn't it?" For Oscar, the environment of Jamestown seemed odd initially.

In fact, since I had resided in Manhattan for nearly a decade before I started to date Oscar in 1989, I too found Jamestown to be a little scary at that point. The fact that there was not a proliferation of beaming streetlights at night or people around who could help if you needed assistance or any kind of protection—such as doormen or guards in front of your home—had become disconcerting. The wide spaces, dark woods, and solitude could be unsettling for me. I had adjusted to New York City life in such a way that rural America seemed threatening, not the other way around.

Over the years, though, our feelings about both New York City and my hometown changed quite a bit. After Oscar had visited New York State's Southern Tier more often, he came to see the virtues of the area with greater discernment and appreciation. Likewise, he acknowledged the benefits of growing up in such an idyllic region.

More and more often, I would hear wistful comments such as this: "Wow, it must have been great for you being a kid in this nice place. Everything is so peaceful." Our house was in a wooded, well-kept area on a cul-de-sac.

By 2013, both Oscar and I were less enthusiastic about New York City living with its endless construction, constant noise, and frenetic pace. It had begun taking its toll on our souls, and we were thinking of spending more time in our lovely, quiet Connecticut town of Branford, an ideal New England village in our estimation. Oscar wanted to buy a house of our own that he could call a "parsonage."

This yet-to-be-found manse would have a large room with glassed-in wall shelves for Oscar's enormous and alluring vintage lead collectible figures of Britains, Mignot, Heide, and Vertunni craftsmanship: French soldiers, Roman warriors and chariots, playful clowns, figurines depicting country life, little animals and not-so-little animals such as elephants, flower gardens, trees, castles, and bridges. A collection that meant much to him because it inspired all sorts of imaginary travels and triumphs, unusual circumstances, and historical moments of import. He had been collecting and storing box upon box of amazing lead treasures for years, and he anticipated their artful placement in a future home to be gazed upon.

As for me, the vision of a parsonage meant an opportunity to create a small flower and herb garden, an English garden you might say, where we could sit, hold hands, talk literature, and watch the sun set. It conjured an image of a home of simple beauty and plain ways—no fuss, no fancy belongings—where we could entertain family and friends in a setting of tranquility.

I especially longed for a kitchen where I didn't have to worry about keeping everything polished and perfect. I wanted to be able to cut vegetables on the counter without caring if there were scratches and gouges afterward, take down a pot hanging from the ceiling, and pull a utensil from a big earthenware crock on a rough-hewn table. A true, working kitchen, the kind you might find in a kindly English farmhouse.

The notion of owning a house played out as a game. It became our focus whenever we found ourselves a bit restless in our Connecticut place on the shore.

Oscar: "Let's take a drive this afternoon to look for our parsonage."

Me: "Great. Should we drive toward The Thimble Islands? Stony Creek? We can stop at Taken for Granite. I saw an ottoman there I really want to buy. And I need candles."

Oscar: "Sure. But let's take the back road. I want to look at that stone house on Route 146 again. Don't you think it's perfect?"

Me: "Well, it's gorgeous, yes. But it's way too big. It has a ballroom!"

Oscar, with a grin: "A ballroom that could be transformed into a display room and library."

A Little Christmas

Today I hear the Jamestown High School A Cappella Choir practicing in the sanctuary. They are rehearsing for their annual Christmas programs, which are presented on several December Sunday afternoons in the nave of First Church. They are singing parts of Handel's *Messiah,* an opus that can truly take me away from this earth to the stars.

It is Advent as I write these pages, and I am remembering Christmases past during my courtship with Oscar and the many beautiful, sacred Yuletide days we observed throughout our marriage.

From the very start, when we began to date in the summer of 1989—six years after we had first met and become friends—we would talk about our understanding of God and eternity. These subjects were at the center of our lives together. I think it was our second date that defined how moving forward in our relationship would work. I told Oscar that I had been raised faithfully (my mother had taught Sunday School, and my father had been on the church council; I had assisted in teaching Bible school a few summers) and that the Lord had guided me throughout my days, even as a young girl in elementary school. *I knew things,* I told him. What I was trying to say is that from the earliest stage of my existence I had felt a special understanding of who I was and where I was supposed to go. I possessed what the medieval philosopher Maimonides referred to as "a spiritual perception."

Oscar, for his part, was influenced greatly by his Catholic roots and early education. He explained to me that he had gone to Catholic elementary school, Corpus Christi, on the Upper West Side of New York, in Morningside Heights. He had profound attachments to Catholicism and reverence for the teachings he had received as a child. He was deeply respectful of the church, especially the Sinsinawa nuns who had been so kind to him when he was a little boy having to navigate an immigrant household. (They gave him his first truly American treat: a peanut butter and jelly sandwich. He loved the iconic snack so much that he asked me to make it for him every birthday of his life while we were married.) But, and this is noteworthy about my husband's devotion, he was not one who attended mass nor did he discuss the depth of his faith in public, although on occasion, at a swanky dinner party or a black-tie affair, he would defend churchgoing Christians and "believing in God" with remarkable elan. Essentially, he preferred to channel his religious ideas and feelings into his fictional work. In the following excerpt from *Blue Antiquity*, Oscar sums up perfectly the duality of his deep faith and the presentation of it in his daily life in the protagonist Mercado.

> As one of those hands who turned up at the Academy's villa from time to time, most usually during the summers, Mercado was of that ilk of enterprising scholar whose frequent visits there over the years had more to do with the fact that he was far better appreciated among his colleagues as a can-do archeologist who really knew his way around a dig, than for any particular academic savoir faire. A Christ specialist, in that for years he had written articles and monographs on different aspects of early Christian life, and whose City College dissertation, circa 1985, had been entitled *On the Pagan Roots of Christianity,* he had occasionally surprised the more serious academics with his good-natured (wine-fueled) contention that yes, indeed, not only did he believe in God, but that, in his opinion, the historical figure known as Jesus, however mythologized, surely possessed certain mystical powers and could have escaped his fate, had He wanted to; and that the Resurrection, in some sense at least, had taken place—surely, if not His Flesh, His Spirit, as a holograph perhaps, had appeared to others: why would anyone have bothered to make that up? And why had that event, as recorded in the gospels, persuaded so many and for so long—unless it were true? Since Mercado was younger when he first made such arguments, more seasoned academics, classicists and historians alike, had looked the other way, never making more than a congenial attempt at rebuttal, even when they could point to the inventive nature of

Christianity, while privately musing that Mercado, so bright a young man, was gravely and perhaps neurotically mistaken.

(To boot, he had attended City College, after all.)

Even the priests from the pontifical institute, Jesuits and Marists alike, and wonderful drinkers all, found his discourses somewhat alarming, for as much as they believed in their mission they, deep down, saw the history of Jesus and his teachings as a predominantly moral movement, the scuttlebutt of miracle making and the wonders performed by the messiah and saints who followed him, more in the nature of an ongoing publicity campaign rather than anything that could ever—or should ever—be proven, for men, so mortal and short-lived, needed their hopes.

Above all, Mercado, or at least some part of him, truly believing that "something" colossal existed behind the universe ("Call it God, if you like"), took it personally if someone disagreed with him, and such folks far outnumbered him. Particularly his brethren in archeology, for whom the earth was but a sepulcher of the illustrious dead, and whose constant encounters with the buried past, from ancient bones to ladles, made the notion of an afterlife, and physical resurrection, an absurdity. Intellectually speaking, Mercado was not far behind them, but if he clung to and pursued, and doggedly so, his beliefs, he did so out of a loyalty to his roots, and, truth be told, his social class. When a scholar dismissed Christian faith as wishful thinking, or as a product of ignorance, he became incensed as if his own family—his mother in particular, and so many generations of believers before her for that matter—had been accused of being dupes, or had been scammed, as they'd say in his old neighborhood.

The number of times, in earlier years, in which he had stormed off from a dinner table, at the Academy and elsewhere, feeling truly offended by the way someone had looked at him, or rolled his eyes when Mercado had made one of his all-encompassing and (to most rational folks) embarrassing statements about the existence of the soul (which he truly did believe) or that in terms of chops, one either had it or didn't when it came to religion, were innumerable. It simply pissed him off to be around people who didn't allow for the possibility of God, and he, feeling himself cast as some kind of naive Santa-Claus-in-the-Clouds fool, had, through his stance, made fewer friends within the academic world than if he had simply accepted the equal likelihood of their point of view.

On the other hand, Mercado didn't have much patience for the marriage of church and politics in America, for Evangelists who preached country music--filled heavens, and, if the truth be told, for overly self-righteous Catholics, or for those who skimmed that faith along the surface, an attitude which at least explained his longings for the depth of conviction once professed by his simple Cuban mother and her friends, to whom Jesus and the sacraments really meant something.

* * *

Nevertheless, attending Mass in her company toward the end of her days, while somewhat comforting in a nostalgic way, for during certain moments of the services a whiff of incense could still take him deeply back to the time of his life when he believed that God was everywhere—as if He were an immense forest, the swallows circling in the violet sky, the very breathing earth on which he walked—Mercado tended to feel that those outings were really a waste of his time; and such rituals, as his mother lighting a candle, in memory of her own late mother in Cuba, before a statue of the Virgin, quaint and, yes, superstitious. (In that, he often thought, his mother wasn't too different from an ancient Roman making an offering to a god.) It was she who had taught him to pray; to venerate the name of Jesus; and to never think selfishly of himself—"Consider the spirit of *El Senor*, and His son, in his *sufrimientos*, instead"; that, above all, he had an immortal soul. He once so truly believed in such things that for years he could not walk past a church without making a sign of the cross—secretly, if some jive street toughs were on hand to watch—and well into his teens he carried both a scapular and a rosary hidden in his pockets, as if he were an aspiring Saint Stephen in the time of Diocletian's persecution. For years he swore that he had actually once seen an incarnation of the Star of Bethlehem as a boy, from his stoop on 123rd Street, which looked westward up a steep hill toward the spires of Riverside Church. There, floating in the night sky, and with its aureole amplified by an aberration in the atmosphere, either a star like Polaris or the planet Venus glowed so large and bright that he took it as a sign that God was winking at him. (This, of course, he kept to himself, but even decades later, when out at an excavation in a remote place, like Sardis in Turkey, where the stars were dazzling at night, he, despite its improbability, still sometimes wondered if he had seen the real thing.)

The late fall of 1989, a season that would nurture our intense transition from friends to lovers, led to our first Christmas together. And that Christmas was all about finding the perfect tree.

We began our search in the late afternoon, as the night sky grabbed away the opalescent light of a frigid day. Oscar was wrapped more warmly than I. He always wore mittens or gloves in the winter, a woolen cap, and a heavy jacket. He was particularly sensitive to freezing temperatures. Having grown up in Western New York, in the snow belt, I was more careless about the cold. It didn't bother me. No hat, no gloves.

Hand in hand, we started our jaunt up Broadway, beginning at my apartment building on 80th and Amsterdam.

There were tree stands galore on nearly every block. And Oscar was determined to stop at each one. It was magical and fun for me because I had never shopped for a Christmas tree in Manhattan. Having been single since arriving in the city, I had always made do with visiting the towering evergreen at Rockefeller Center and calling it my own. Just like every other New Yorker who loved Christmas.

At our first stop I found what I considered to be the perfect specimen. Not too tall, not too full. Just right by my estimation. But, no, Oscar thought that we could do much better. "Let's keep going," he said with a smile.

The next stop was twice as large as the first with, of course, many more trees and wreaths, swags, and stands.

This pop-up was overseen by a mirthful Canadian who sang a little bit and joked around. The jolly proprietor was to Oscar's liking and soon the two of them were engaged in stories about Christmas and memories of childhood. There was nothing Oscar liked more than to engage a stranger, any stranger, in a conversation about his or her life and all the particulars. (In fact, this is one of the ways Oscar did research for character development in his novels. He bombarded people with questions to cull the essence of their psyches and their spirits. Then he stored this information in his memory to use when the time was right.)

The amiable merchant and Oscar were enjoying their chat so much that buying a Fraser fir had become a secondary goal. So, off I went on my own, sniffing around and dragging trees out of their bundles, getting pricked and bruised until Oscar appeared at my side with a huge grin. "This man is hip. He has great stories."

"Hey," I answered. "What do you think of this one?" I was holding a sappy pine by its trunk and smiling hopefully.

"Nice. It's really nice. But I think we can find something better," he answered, waving toward the next block.

And so, we trudged under the canopy of little white lights that connected one tree stand to another.

We investigated tree stand after tree stand, roamed block after block until we got to Oscar's neighborhood on West 106th Street. We had, by that time, stopped at twelve tree vendor sites. I was curious about Oscar's reluctance to purchase any number of nice candidates and started to think that maybe he really didn't want to buy a tree that night. Maybe, I thought, this was just a practice run. But then, out of the blue, Oscar said, "Lori, there is one more stand I want to see on Amsterdam. Okay?"

"Of course," I answered, relieved that maybe we would get our tree after all.

We turned right on Broadway and walked the long block leading to our last destination on Amsterdam Avenue.

There, on the northwest corner of the intersection, was an old man wearing a very thin coat, standing next to an assortment of three trees, all of which were spindly, small, and sad. Without hesitating, Oscar grabbed the least of the lot and said to me, "Isn't it just perfect? I knew we would find the best tree here." He handed the man one hundred dollars, placed the tree on his right shoulder, and put his left arm around my waist. We turned south toward his apartment. "Mil gracias, señor," said the vendor under his breath as we stepped away.

It was then, that very moment, that Oscar planted himself in my heart for good.

Sudden Fame, Consequences

When Oscar published *The Mambo Kings Play Songs of Love* in 1989—just weeks after our first date—its immediate and overwhelming success was unexpected. Yes, his agent and his editor and a small group of allies, including me, had read the novel with awe and excitement; we knew that it was a masterwork. The novel was a thrilling tour de force of originality, style, and execution. No one had written anything like it in the history of American literature. There was something in the sprawling, heartbreaking, lavish, and sexy read for just about everyone: Spanish lyricism, erotic fervor, spiritual depth, a capacious story about the American dream, and the wrenching reality of the immigrant's existence (the annealing element of true Americana). When I read it in galleys, I did so in one sitting, propped up in my bed. I began the book in the early evening and finished it just before I headed out the door to work the following morning. I devoured it in a kind of trance. I could not believe the novel's beauty, power, and ripping effect on my heart. I didn't know if I had read a kind of Old Testament story in a postmodern New York City frame or if I had just read the most transformative novel I had ever consumed since *Don Quixote*. The style was dizzyingly unique; the emotional air of its story made me catch my breath. I believed that I was a different person having read the book. Tears streamed down my cheeks the whole way through. I realized that Oscar was the stylist I had been waiting to discover in contemporary letters. A true literary genius. And I was totally fascinated about something else: I realized that he had done something unique in American writing. He had been able to show how Judeo-Christian faith embraced and celebrated the totality of humanness, including the sexual side of a human being. Ashamed of our sexual nature? Oscar was saying no, and embracing sexuality as a God-given gift. I am reminded of a New Testament story put forth in the book of Luke 7:36–50. There is pure eroticism in the act of the woman, identified by some scholars as a certain Mary, sister of Martha, who anoints Jesus's bare feet with perfume and tears in this passage. Does Jesus object to this over-the-top act of love and adoration? No. Quite simply, there is a blending of selflessness and sexuality in this gift to Jesus, which he accepts wholeheartedly.

Oscar's description of lovemaking was bold, unabashed, and gleeful. I am bemused when a high-minded critic tells me that the novel is "machista." I believe such thinking is cramped, facile—and mistaken—and so did Oscar. To read and comprehend *The Mambo Kings* is to understand how Oscar, as an artist, as an innovative novelist, was showing certain truths about the stereotypical Cuban macho. He was, in effect, turning long-held ideas upside down (he was ribbing the macho figure and revealing the female "target" for her smarts, resourcefulness, and, in some cases, unabashed appetites). Oscar was challenging stale and traditional attitudes about ardor. And...surprise...he often said to interviewers that he thought *The Mambo Kings* was "a very religious novel." What he meant by this is the work distilled humanity to its essence of memory, compassion, mercy, and redemption.

Something more about Oscar's landmark book. None of us in his little support circle had any idea that *The Mambo Kings* would become an international bestseller. In fact, Oscar's publishing team had taken pains to dampen his expectations for any kind of success. They accurately explained to him that, in 1980s America, little attention was given to "Hispanic" books. The critics weren't interested in themes associated with Spanish-speaking citizens, and neither were the small number of readers who did respond to literary fiction. It was almost as if anything relating to Latino culture caused an allergy among critics and readers alike.

This is why Oscar decided to go abroad (specifically, Portugal) the summer *The Mambo Kings* was being released. He wanted to get far away from the impending publication and any kind of deflation or disappointment he might be facing. The disheartening silence of rejection and dismissal for many novelists, if not most, can be devastating after spending years of toil on its creation.

Often being a novelist means: work with no pay-out. No pats on the back, either.

The Mambo Kings, Oscar's second expedition into the realm of writing novels, exemplified his commitment to his chosen path as an artist, but by no means augured any notions of grandeur or financial reward. He was an incredibly hard worker, and he saw his future as one of artistic sacrifice, with possibly enough luck "to pay the bills." Yes, after being awarded the Rome Prize for *Our House in the Last World*, Oscar did leave his steady management position at an advertising agency that highly regarded him, but it wasn't because he was sure of future writing success; it was because he had been given enough positive feedback from a few critics and overseers in publishing to make the risk of trying to survive as a novelist worth it. He decided to take a part-time teaching job at Hofstra University in the evenings, in addition to writing full time. The Rome Prize had convinced him that he might just be able to scrape by as a novelist. In other words, he wanted to live by doing something he loved to do, something he was born to do, even if it meant living from hand-to-mouth.

Both of our lives changed forever with the publication of *The Mambo Kings Play Songs of Love* and its eventual selection for the Pulitzer Prize in 1990. For Oscar it was a miracle. One minute he was a struggling, albeit admired, up-and-coming novelist, and the next he was an international literary star. The global rights to the novel were being sold in rapid succession. A movie based on the book was in the works. Invitations to travel all over the country and all over the world were nonstop. Harriet Wasserman, Oscar's agent at the time, was calling every hour to inform us that yet another TV commentator wished to interview Oscar. Major radio talk show hosts were clamoring to talk to him. Celebrities in the film world, music industry, and show business sometimes camped out in the lobby of Oscar's building, waiting to meet him and talk art and music. There was a sudden mambo craze at jazz clubs throughout the city. It seemed everyone wanted to learn how to master this iconic, sensual Cuban dance.

For me, this overwhelming interest in Oscar and his book was exciting and extremely stressful. I was absolutely elated for Oscar and for the extraordinary reception he and his novel were getting. But at the same time, we had just started to seriously date, and I wanted to have quiet time with him. Now that was nearly impossible. There were book tours galore, weekend engagements, and constant invitations to international conferences and symposia. The focus on Oscar could be overwhelming. The sudden celebrity, perhaps, sounds thrilling, but there were all sorts of difficulties that went along with this kind of literary fame and public exposure, not least of them trying to maintain my energy and sense of self-worth.

I rose to the challenge, however lonely and embattled I might have felt sometimes. Oscar was the soulmate I had been waiting for, so I had to find a way to support him and build upon our fledgling love, come what may. And I suppressed my own feelings of being left behind and sometimes mistreated by strangers (early on in our courtship, I once overheard a female festival organizer say in my direction: "She's just the girlfriend, not his wife"). I realized that this was the crucial moment of our lives, and that it called for every ounce of my intellect and spiritual will to be sustained. So, you could say that well before the official, legal ceremony of wedlock—eight years before, to be exact—our marriage was forged in those days of coming to grips with massive upheaval and a stardust social scene that neither one of us had experienced before.

Wrapped in Music

"WHAT INCREDIBLE MUSIC. What is that? It's beautiful," mused my editor, Marc Aronson, who had called to ask a question about a book of mine that he was editing.

"Hmm, not sure," I answered. I didn't know because Oscar had stacked the CDs in the sound system of the back room of our apartment before he left for his studio that morning, and I hadn't been around to see the names of the musical ensembles and composers of those recordings. I didn't recognize the musician whose work was filling every space of our airy home and served as accompaniment to my musings. "I suspect it is someone you and I never heard of," I commented. "Oscar loves obscure compositions, especially from Central Asia and Africa." I was proud of his vast and discerning knowledge of musical repertoire.

Oscar loved all styles of composition. He reveled in the mastery of the great classical artists (Bach was número uno) to the Romantic nineteenth-century wonders (Fauré and Respighi come to mind, especially); he was hip to the jazz giants from North and Latin America, such as Bill Evans; and was thrilled by classical guitarists, pianists of every genre, blues and soul, rock, Renaissance antiphonal arrangements, and every orientation of religious offering thinkable. In the Christian vein, he especially felt close to Palestrina. He was partial to the joyous mayhem of church bells, too.

"It's wonderful," decided Marc. "Just amazing."

I could have said the same of Oscar's musical soul. His love of music and the way it infiltrated and affected his life and work was elemental to understanding him. Not only was he a self-taught musician, but he was constantly challenging himself to learn more about music and unusual instruments, and he pushed to grow as a practitioner of jazz piano (his devil-may-care approach always brought smiles to my face) at the baby grand Knabe in our living room.

Oscar's fans across the globe, of course, know that he celebrated the "mambo" and brought it to the high table of literature, but the truth is that Oscar celebrated rhythm in all his work, from his first novel, *Our House in the Last World,* to *Blue Antiquity*.

Oscar's prose was orchestral, symphonic, from the bold way he arranged his sentences to the swelling momentum of the arc of his chapters. Each book that sprung from Oscar's desk was a lyrical composition set to his own demanding ear. Sound in writing was essential to him. And sometimes, when describing an especially pleasing turn of phrase, he would enact it physically, turning his face toward me with an uplifted chin, a click of his tongue, and his hands in the air as if he were about to conduct his own words.

He used to recount how, as a child of five or six, he would hide in a living room corner, or under the kitchen table, and watch his parents and their friends dance in their railroad apartment on West 118th Street. He loved the raucous rhythms that his parents favored, as well as the sweet, romantic ballads, such as "En Mi Viejo San Juan," that his mother liked to sing during the day as Oscar was recovering from nephritis as a little boy.

Then, it was the traditional Cuban beats and strains of his parents' homeland that would captivate his heart and propel him toward imagining "la Isla." But as Oscar grew up and assumed the persona of a hip inner-city youth, his tastes ran to rock and jazz. He was precocious and easily processed information about what was happening musically on the streets, on Columbia University's campus where his family's apartment was located, and in friends' homes and coffee shops in the Village. He was becoming a lover of melodic exposition and practice.

His passion for music was alive to such a degree that, having desired a piano—an instrument that his parents could not afford—he was on the lookout for a way to have one...for free. In the way things often came to Oscar—from the supernatural—he eventually found his piano on the sidewalk in front of his house.

One of the earliest tales Oscar lovingly shared with me of his young adult days was that of "the grand piano." A grand piano that someone had abandoned on the sidewalk smack in front of his apartment building. Did its owner find the instrument too rickety and beyond-repair to keep? Did it come from a basement beset by mold? Did an elderly music professor, from the nearby Manhattan School of Music, pass away without instructions for its disposal? Did the piano simply not fit into a moving truck when its owner was suddenly transferred to another city? Neither Oscar nor his parents knew the answer. All that Oscar truly understood was that he *wanted* that piano.

Day after day, Oscar looked through the living room window of his apartment to see if the treasure had been taken. Day after day, the answer was: no. There it waited patiently to be claimed. So, after a week—a safe enough time to assume that the piano was there for the taking—he dragged and hauled it to the top of the building's stoop. Repeated attempts to get it through the door came to nothing until he had the idea to deconstruct the body. He ran inside, took some tools that his Pop kept in a closet, and rushed back out with the help of a friend to claim the prize as his own. Cutting off a little here and a little there, the piano finally sailed through the portal handily. And then Oscar put the object of his affection back together, piece by piece.

Playing the piano was an ardent desire then, when he was just a boy, and it would be a mainstay of his life through trial, tribulation, and triumph until the day he died. He had, in fact, played our baby grand Knabe the day before he passed away, and the complex sheet music he had been studying stayed in place for eleven years until I sold our apartment. I couldn't touch it. I gave our piano to a residence for the elderly a few blocks away from our co-op a month before I left our home forever.

But even more than piano, Oscar loved the guitar. He owned quite a few, as well as a mandolin and a Cuban Tres. He cared deeply for these truly beautiful instruments and made sure that they were regularly hydrated (with little tubes of water placed within the sound holes). He showed off his favorite Spanish guitar on a stand in the living room.

At Christmastime Oscar loved to accompany me singing carols on that exquisitely fashioned Spanish guitar, the perfect ending to a full day of decorating our tree with ornaments from around the world.

Rosemary

THIS MORNING THERE IS A THIN LAYER of snow on the ground. It is a humid, gray December day, the kind of common winter day in this region of the country I remember from my youth. Contrary to what might seem a normal reaction to a frosty clime, bitter cold, and a dreary sky, I love it. This is my favorite season. Winter in all its starkness and simplicity. A cut-out in natural splendor. Oscar loved winter too, especially the snow that comes with it in the Northeast.

My eye catches the Bob Bragg pergola in the church's community garden, and I look for the apple tree behind it as well as the herb borders of rosemary, thyme, basil, and parsley. I see that the rosemary and thyme are still growing, abundant and fragrant even in the frozen earth. I stop by the sidewalk and pull hard on a bush. A tiny rosemary sprig is in my right hand, and I crush it to release the scent. I breathe in the earthy, pungent, pine-like oils as they fill the air. Memories of Rome hit me hard.

I remember, particularly, the blissful days that Oscar and I spent at the American Academy on the Janiculum Hill, in the neighborhood of Monteverde, overlooking the Vatican. Even though they were incredibly beautiful sojourns, Oscar could become deeply nostalgic and a bit wistful when we were in his old environs. This excerpt has Mercado ruminating on the passage of time, just as Oscar would:

> Walking through Monteverde, a neighborhood that in ancient times had been a senatorial summer retreat, as he'd look around, at traffic, the internet cafes and tanning salons, a kind of stepping back in time happened: it was not hard for him to imagine a two-horse chariot wheeling by alongside him, slaves bearing loads following behind, en route to a Roman villa overlooking the ancient city, perhaps along the promontory now known as la Via Garibaldi. It was the sort of fantasy he'd always entertained as a younger man, when, aside from his visions of rising to great heights as an archeologist and scholar, which never quite happened, he often imagined things as they had once been.
>
> In fact, coming in from the airport, nothing cheered Mercado more than his first view through a taxi window of the Colosseum for that road took him by the Forum, that great and haunted graveyard of stone and marble, whose grounds, teeming with mists and whispers in the early mornings, he knew well, the sight of so many columns and sacred

temple ruins, resurrected from the medieval garbage dump and shepherd's pasture they had once been buried under, always warming his heart. To the west, rising above the ancient center, the Palatine Hill and Nero's villa, umbrella pines, shrubbery and wisteria vines hanging over the bluff. Once, as a dapper white-gloved policeman, in an outlandishly stylish dark blue uniform and pith helmet, presided over the tangle of honking automobiles, busses and *motorini* along the Via Cavour, Mercado became fixated on the sunlight overwhelming the avenue ahead of him, to where the buildings receded into a glare of burning whiteness; suddenly the pedestrians, students, and tourists thronging the sidewalks, seemed as ethereal as phantoms, their whitewashed forms casting behind them shadows that, stretching into the distance, seemed to have slipped through time; in such moments, it was not hard for Mercado to imagine, if only for a split second, that he was getting a glimpse of second-century Rome.

But what was he to do? No matter how often he tried not to think about the past, it seemed to hound him anyway. Indeed, as much as he liked to imagine it otherwise, time went on and on its merry way and all too quickly. Down by the open-air market, just of *la via Fratelli Bonetti*, where he'd inevitably stop en route back to the academy, it always killed him to see how much the sexy and buxom teenager he once doted on had changed: the same shapely girl who, to her burly wart-nosed father's consternation, had worn too-tight blouses and always handled the stall's ripe melons and succulent peaches as provocatively as might a nymph,

> even going so far sometimes as to roll her tongue over her lower lip while holding up a piece of plump fruit and saying, *"E molto saporoso."* It killed him to see that over the years she too turned burly and wart-nosed herself; a female Jekyll and Hyde transformation that enhanced Mercado's own curmudgeonly stance that something about his own life had gone amiss. Or as his mantra went, Donald Duck books and the small pleasures of his existence aside, if only he'd known how quickly time slipped by, oh the things he would have done differently.

The magnificent American Academy in Rome sits in the middle of grounds that can make a visitor swoon. So spectacular are the gardens, fountains, and edifices dating back hundreds of years that walking through the compound feels as if one has left reality and entered an otherworldly realm of glory and serenity. In the following excerpt from *Blue Antiquity*, Mercado sums up the grounds like this:

> Through the Academy's back gardens he walked, the Aurelian walls to one side, a row of apricot trees on the other, birds chirping and piano music pouring out one of the composer's studios, a sixteenth-century domicile, called *la casa rustica*, where it had been said that Galileo had once stayed. Before him, surrounded by umbrella pine trees, the splendid academy grounds that with each passing year seemed far less rustic than he recalled from his youthful days, its lawns far better trimmed than before, his favorite trellis, heavy with grapes, which had covered the path halfway from the back gate to the academy rear entrance, and off which

> it was so easy to pick a handful of such plump and delicious *uve* from overhead, long since taken down. The very path from the back gate itself, of deeply inset stone and rubble, often muddy and running after a rain, had been in recent years replaced by a country club-style array of roundish flagstones, a pain, however pleasant looking, to walk on and by his lights, not anywhere near as charming.

But Rome, for us, was much more than the Academy. We took the opportunity every day to explore every bit of the city as much as we could. Our varied and long walks took us all over the cobble-stoned streets, with Campo de' Fiori (we were always on the lookout for *tarocchi* or blood oranges), Piazza Navona (we would sit and talk about Bernini and Borromeo while pondering the magnificence of their fountains), the Giudecca (the carciofi alla guidia to die for!), the Aventine Hill (one sublime cathedral after another and the wonderful shops selling creams and oils made by the monks were mandatory visits), and Testaccio being our favorite haunts along with the grounds of the Forum.

Oscar loved churches of all kinds. He particularly loved the cathedrals and chapels of Rome. On any given day we probably stopped at no fewer than three. Every time we walked down to Trastevere from the Janiculum Hill we visited Santa Maria, which means we went there as part of our daily routine. I don't think there was a church that meant more to him for sentimental reasons than this exquisite, ancient house of worship. After walking the aisles and sitting for a while in one of the pews, we would always visit the little shop of trinkets and booklets before heading out for a cappuccino across from the piazza and then lunch at Da Paris, our favorite haunt around the corner.

Tagine

I DON'T KNOW WHY but Oscar's TV appearances always seemed to be scheduled for Monday mornings. These were not the easiest times. The nerves and anticipation of being interviewed—by, let's say, Bryant Gumbel on the *Today* show, Pat Mitchell for CBS, or in later years, Don Lemon for CNN and Ray Suarez on behalf of PBS, or someone equally notable on another network—was a bit unsettling for Oscar.

In the early days, that is during our courtship, I resorted to cooking a romantic meal on Sunday evenings at my place to calm us down. The first meal I ever made for Oscar was a kind of slapdash coq au vin. It was about the only delicious main course I thought I prepared reasonably well.

Oscar had cooked for me on our third date. And because his linguini with artichokes and pancetta had been so very good, I deduced that food might be quite important to him. I was not wrong. In getting to know one another better, he explained that his father, Pascual, had made a living in the '50s and '60s by cooking at the now-defunct Biltmore Hotel in New York City. Often Pascual would invite his little son into the establishment's industrial kitchen and show him the ropes. This is how, at age six, Oscar had learned the difference between German and Dutch bitter chocolate, an esoteric distinction that I, as an adult, was not able to make.

Now, looking back on my methods, it is a wonder I thought my chicken in wine would appeal to a man with as sophisticated a palate as Oscar's, a man who had spent several years living and writing in Rome and had honed his culinary flair in the environs of Trastevere.

But it was Oscar who sparked my interest in cuisine. It had been a minor concern for me once I had become totally devoted to literature, writing, and a rigorous New York City professional life in my twenties. Like so many of my friends, I preferred going out to restaurants for a meal because there was such a variety of excellent and intriguing places to try, from Ethiopian to Armenian.

My husband's love of food restored my youthful interest in the culinary arts. I especially liked to make familiar Italian dishes like stuffed peppers, eggplant parmigiana, and chicken cacciatore. But I also learned to make a few of Oscar's favorite Cuban dishes: ropa vieja, picadillo, and arroz con pollo. I prepared a lot of Spanish meals as well, such as fideos, tortilla española, paella, and ensalada rusa. Oscar liked these sorts of homey and comforting meals.

From the large window in my bright, little kitchen I could watch old men standing around telling stories and kids riding their bikes in front of the Cuban bodega directly across the street. Salsa blared from open windows. I learned to make what became one of Oscar's favorite Sunday supper meals—simple spaghetti in meat sauce—to the beat of Willie Colón.

Oscar's mother, when she would meet with me for coffee and spicy storytelling, would stress that Oscar's good health depended on low-salt, fat-free, and bland foods. His childhood nephritis had badly compromised his physical health long ago, she would explain, and he had been told since boyhood by doctors that he would not live a long life. She reminded me of these conditions again and again. Eating fat-free food was a must for him. Whenever she warned me of this situation, I would tune her out because the last thing on earth I wanted to hear was that the man I had fallen in love with so passionately and completely would not live to be an old man. Little did Magdalena know that he rarely observed the mandate of fat-free food if given the choice on a night out at a restaurant or at a fancy dinner party courtesy of an extravagant host. I did, however, try my hardest to do exactly as Magda dictated whenever I cooked, which was often. I broiled a lot of fish and a lot of skinless chicken. I used very little fat in any of my recipes. Olive oil, yes, but never butter.

Oscar could be indulgent when it came to food selections. One of his absolute loves was the oily, crispy rind of Cuban roasted pork, otherwise known as the crackly crust or *cuero de pernil.* His favorite go-to meal was chicken—any kind of chicken *with* skin. But he especially liked two preparations: roast chicken and chicken tagine. The former I made reasonably well, but I became expert in the latter.

A two-part trip, one that began in Morocco and ended in the French Riviera, initiated my study of chicken tagine and its correct preparation. No one taught me how to make this perfect dish; I learned by memory of taste, presentation, aroma, and trial and error, after we returned home to New York City. I think I made it fifteen times in my kitchen before I landed on the exact equation of fowl, preserved lemon, olives, condiments, and spices. And because it wasn't feasible for me to make the recipe in the traditional, earthenware conical vessel—literally the *tagine*—I learned to prepare it in another kind of American-made clay and ceramic baking dish, which worked surprisingly well.

We first tasted this amazing, iconic Moroccan delight in Marrakesh in a very old, romantic restaurant in the kasbah. The setting of our meal was just as impressive as the repast. The most amazing, tiled room of mirrors, indigo ceramics, dizzying white plasterwork known as *yeseria*, and candlelight. Straight out of *Arabian Nights*.

When I saw the look on Oscar's face as he took his first bite of this delectable dish, I knew that I would have to learn how to make it. The reason is quite simple: giving Oscar a good meal at the end of the day mattered more to me than almost anything else I did in our domestic life. Writing novels was so demanding of his spirit, mind, and body that eating a better-than-average supper was a *must* for emotional balance. A better-than-average dinner could change Oscar's mood from dark to light in a flash.

Routines and Breaking Them

IF I WERE TO DESCRIBE my husband's writing routine, I would have to use the word *disciplined* to start. Oscar was exceedingly hardworking. A typical day went like this for him: Arise at 7:30 AM, eat breakfast by 8:00, retire to the study to read, think, or watch a bit of an old movie—something of the latter by one of his favorite directors such as Preston Sturges, William Wyler, Alfred Hitchcock, or Billy Wilder—and then go to the office. He wrote from 9:00 or 9:30 AM until 8:00 PM. Every day we were in New York City this was how his day was divided. We had two homes initially, and then in later years three: one in Connecticut and one in Durham, North Carolina besides our place on the Upper West Side of Manhattan. His daily schedule would vary depending on the location, especially when we were in Connecticut. We took many more time-outs during the work day because Killam's Point was our summer vacation home. Oscar might take an extra swim, depending on the hour of high tide, for instance. Sometimes he would spend a few hours reading comics ("Hey, Lor, some men read *Playboy*: I read Donald Duck!") or he would engage in a household chore with gusto. We often went for a leisurely lunch at our favorite Italian restaurant, Assaggio, in Branford's little village square. And we always ordered the same dishes: chicken scarpariello for Oscar, grilled Chilean sea bass for me.

Because he worked nearly round the clock most of the year, I wrote almost as much. But I had found that keeping track of our frenetic schedule of book tours, receptions, speaking engagements, openings of one sort or another, and endless international trips occupied my time considerably. And I also wanted to cook healthy meals for him. So, while I devoted about three or four hours a day to research and writing, I spent much of my day attending to these other duties. I loved the kitchen, and I was always trying to replicate the delicious dishes that we had eaten in far-flung parts of the globe. And cooking helped to relax me.

A stranger at a reading that Oscar and I gave together one evening in New York City pulled me aside during the reception afterward and said, "I can see that the two of you are a real team. You two are a powerful duo." Few people, perhaps, understand that a major writer needs a strong partner. A very dear friend put it another way. He offered this as a summation of who Oscar and I were, a few months after Oscar passed: "The two of you were a double helix." I loved this description because it so poetically captured the essence of our being. Our spirits were intertwined to such a degree that we knew if something were to happen to one of us...the other would have a hellish time going on. While this sentiment is held by many committed and loving couples, I think what made us slightly different is the fact that our work was often collaborative and all-consuming. We wrote nearly every day of the year, except for Christmas Day and the days when we fell sick. Even a vacation was about "research" for work. I was so involved in Oscar's creative process, and he was so interested in what I was writing, that we were inseparable—not clingy but always within each other's orbit all day long and available for counsel. We asked each other questions about our work in progress, we depended on each other's acumen to get us beyond an impasse in thought, we needed to hear each other ruminate on this or that aspect of each other's manuscript. And because we didn't have children, we knew that surviving—after either one of our deaths—would lack the necessity of "carrying on" for a son or daughter, no matter what. He occasionally said to me, "If anything happens to you, I don't think I'll make it." And we both often said to each other, "If you die before me, I'll remain alone."

Getting back to our schedules. There were a few times when we abandoned our pretty strict work habits in New York. These were usually instigated by a masterful exhibit at the Met or the launch of a much-anticipated movie.

As films go, Oscar's preference was for older productions shown at various arthouses, retrospectives, or festivals. In this vein some of his favorite all-time productions were *Spartacus*, *Ben-Hur*, *Sullivan's Travels*, *The Magnificent Ambersons*, *The Best Days of Our Lives*, *The Bishop's Wife*, *Lawrence of Arabia*, *King of Kings*, *The*

Apartment, *Black Narcissus*, *Goodbye, Mr. Chips*, *Some Like It Hot*, *Breakfast at Tiffany's*, and *The Thief of Bagdad*. But he always looked forward to a new release, such as *Schindler's List*, *Troy*, *Braveheart*, *Moneyball*, or *Mountains of the Moon*.

We both loved the Metropolitan Museum of Art and to this day I'd have to say that it is my favorite place to visit—anywhere in the world—to get lost in thought and hours of reverie. Oscar's favorite rooms were those dedicated to Greek and Egyptian sculpture and artifacts. If it had been feasible, I believe he would have visited those collections every day of his life.

Oscar did collect antiquities, however, as a consolation. He needed to be surrounded by beauty, he told me, to create.

In *Blue Antiquity*, he references this need by attributing the same to Mercado's mentor, Dr. Hunt, a respected and aristocratic archaeologist/professor. The following could have been written about Oscar's own little collection of treasures:

> Now and then, as well, he'd notice some casually displayed artifact tucked away on a shelf, or sitting atop a cigar box: an Assyrian cylinder seal, an Egyptian *ushabti* a Persian drinking cup, a clay pot from the Holy Land, a dig number scribbled carelessly in marker onto its side. One afternoon when Mercado had been admiring a Persian cup, which bore the image of a bolting stag, Dr. Hunt, no doubt pleased by his interest, called him into an adjacent room, his study. There, he kept a desk, on which sat a manual Olivetti typewriter and papers, and a display case filled with

even more antiquarian items—among them, a tray of (mostly tarnished) Roman coins, a black Etruscan chalice, a cracked puttied-together Greek vase, and, among other things, a mummified Egyptian falcon, all of which Hunt identified as "the random stuff one comes by over the years."

That "stuff," however, amazed Mercado—for they seemed to belong in a museum. Treasure is what he thought of them, and so, he concluded, Hunt must have been a wealthy man. (And he was not wrong in that: for over the years he would learn that archeology attracted its share of intellectually cultivated individuals of means.) But just then Hunt added, "And I mean it when I call this 'stuff.' There's not a thing in this collection that one couldn't find in any bazaar, or respectable antiquarian five-and-dime store." But lest, Mercado, who had, to that point, visited exactly two museums in his life—(The Museum of Natural History and the Metropolitan Museum of Art)—leave that room without seeing the best of what he had, Hunt told him: "But here is one item, which I found some thirty years ago in a creaky old shop in Istanbul, and worth a King's ransom—at least to me."

With that, Hunt opened a closet door; wedged against the corner, behind some hanging clothes, stood a safe, with a combination lock whose cylinders he was soon turning: a click, the door opening, and Hunt, pulling out yet another box, showed Mercado its contents. Unraveled from a wrapping of velvet cloth, a large ring, dense, made of silver and bearing the bull seal and "X" of the Tenth *Fretensis* Legion slipped onto Hunt's palm: "This belonged to one of Titus's generals in Jerusalem, Larcius Lepidus possibly, during the

> sacking of the second temple in 70 AD," Hunt said to Mercado, handing it over to him. "Here, try it on."
>
> The ring, so immense as to have belonged to a giant, accommodated two of Mercado's fingers, which passed easily through its diameter: and its weight was such that Mercado, in a moment of communion with a man who had been dead for nearly two thousand years, imagined that same commander, in an armored breastplate and tasseled helmet, mounted on a horse, his limbs, torso, and head massive: altogether that single ring startled Mercado by how much it conveyed, as if decades of soldiering and warfare and campaigns had been compressed into a single object, much as the sanctity and sufferings of Christ, who had likely died during the general's youth, seemed exemplified in the form of a cross.

Over the years Oscar had acquired a few pieces that gave him a lot of visual pleasure as well as food for thought. He liked first-century Roman artifacts, small utilitarian Etruscan pieces, Egyptian cartonnage masks and burial pieces such as ushabti and ancient glassware and pottery from the Levant. Whenever he acquired an object to add to his little collection, he bought me a piece of jewelry from the same period and region if he could. This is how I have in a special jewelry box necklaces of semi-precious gems such as carnelian and onyx with small silver or bronze beads and clay figurines and ornaments. They are, for the most part, Etruscan. I hardly ever wear them, but I look at the strands often. They were transportive then, while he was alive, and sacred reminders of Oscar's beautiful soul to me, now.

I suppose the most treasured gift of antiquity I received from my husband is a pair of Roman gold earrings dating from 50 CE or thereabouts. They are delicate and remarkable for the quality of the gold identifiable by a honeyed patina. In fact, so captivating are they that when I brought them to a jeweler on Broadway to be slightly reworked so that I could wear them, the shopkeeper stared at me in silence as he held them in his hand. His eyes got wider and wider upon examining them until I asked him why he seemed so startled. "Well, you know this is very old gold. Very, very, very." I smiled and only answered "yes," worrying that if he knew their age, somehow, they might get lost in his care.

Oscar's interest in collecting antiquities was sparked by his love of archaeology as a subject matter and, also, as a kind of vocation. He worked on digs over the years in a yeoman's capacity in diverse parts of the world. This interest began when Oscar first went to Rome as an American Academy fellow in 1986. The following excerpt from *Blue Antiquity* is his fictional reference to this curiosity about the ancient world and the thrill of discovering it through excavation, through digging layer upon layer of earth.

> At the Roman Forum, he had once spent days by the Temple of the Vestal Virgins bringing up clay and carbon samples that dated back to 800 BC, about the time of the first settlements on the Palatine Hill, when the area below consisted of marshlands; then, working alongside a lovely female archeologist, he had gone further down, plunging his tubing deeper and deeper until he hit the bottom of that ancient

lake, the bore filling with sediment dating back fifty thousand years, to the "beginnings of that place," as he had written once. He could identify and roughly date shards from their glaze, weight and thickness, the depths and style of the grooves around their rims; he knew that the appearance of carbon bits in a recess of earth bespoke of a hearth, that animal remains sometimes meant sacrifice to the gods, and how to discern human from animal bone; that the discovery of a stone bench or the marble post holes of an ancient doorway could help define the parameters of a Roman villa from the Republican period or of a *domus rustica* from the times of Augustus; that a pouring rainfall could loosen the ground and bring up out of the earth a bounty of sparkling Roman glass, blackened coins, and pieces of jewelry—diadems and earrings—from long ago.

Arriving at a site, and almost as a reflex, Mercado, taking a look around, could see below the apparent surface. What might appear to a tourist as an ordinarily picturesque Tuscan meadow, with some old broken-down walls and umbrella pines, an uneven indentation or a mound suddenly rising along a plain would loom before Mercado's eyes as a clue to what had been before: a many layered ghost town, part ancient ramparts, or a public square with wells, peristyles and even temples, often overlapping somewhat later structures, medieval foundations or the remains of a tower. Under the right conditions he could see through the brambles, and beyond the ilex and clematis crowding the ground, to where the main causeway into a village had once run or discern just how far into the distance the curvature of a fortification wall extended, or where a stream had once cut through a dense nettle bush to an ancient pool. He'd passed countless hours, crouching in trenches, with a trowel in hand (the archeologist's best friend), carefully scraping away centuries of dirt off a mosaic floor, and, feeling the compacted soil with his palm, could discern the beginnings of a previous level—that point in time where a lower floor had once existed, on which families had slept, babies had crawled, chamber pots had filled, and life had unfolded, so long ago.

He had a reputation for being so good at this that, in years past, more than a few town councils in Italy, longing for an ancient attraction to boost the local tourist trade, had hired Mercado and his crew of students to survey the hills and meadows of their environs for anything, beyond a few lousy coins or a medieval buckler, that might justify the installation of one of those green signs, bearing the white embossed image of a temple, signifying a ruins, along the roads. Lined up in a row at the crest of a hill, they'd sweep downward, probing the ground with rakes, and usually discovering, if anything at all, the remnants of an ancient cemetery or two, not to mention all kinds of more recent debris—tuna fish cans, hunters' shell casings, a rusted spoon, and animal skeletons. (Hardly doing it for the money—a few thousand lire here and there—no matter the outcome, he would be content to preside over a happy wine-soaked, many coursed dinner with his crew in a *trattoria* afterwards, at his employer's expense.)

He'd had several (some thought) dubious successes in that regard—among them a so-called temple of Minerva, the foundations of which he had unearthed at the edge of a withered olive grove, near a dead-end village some twelve miles east of Siena. Though his discovery consisted of nothing more than finding a few partial columns and a pediment on which had been carved Minerva's symbol, an owl, and on which stood the fragment of a slender and shapely foot up to the ankle on one side and another to the knee, the site—(long since turned into a local teenage lover's roost, the marble soon enough became covered with graffiti, as in, "*Ti amo, Cristina, Julio, '97,*" the surrounding grounds littered with candy wrappers and used up condoms)—became a destination for many an unsuspecting traveler. (Which is to say that after making that long meandering drive through farm country, past tomato, zucchini and tomato fields—cicadas buzzing everywhere—visitors tended to find the site less than spectacular.) But near a town called Rimzi, in Lazio, behind centuries worth of garbage that had accumulated along a hillside, tons and tons of it, he and his crew, wearing gloves and covered in head to toe with protective clothing, having cleared the way, found a cave entrance and within it, some yards inside, once the rats, vipers and bats had scattered, some ancient pots and carbon bits, with a few amulets that he identified with the Mithraic cults, as well as some ox bones. This, he speculated, had been a *Tarboleum*, where, in Roman times, Mithraic blood-letting rites had perhaps once taken place—or so that's what he claimed to the local town council. (Without much further ado, or consultation, the cave was henceforth declared a "temple of Mithras.")

Occasionally, while hunting about for some diagnostic materials, he did come across some very interesting things. At a site in Umbria, near Perugia, with a dense brush of thickets to be cleared away by hand, Mercado and his crew of budding archeologists, squatting on their haunches in the July heat, spent a morning pulling out clump after clump of thorny roots and vines over a spot that had been thought to cover a cistern or well. Eventually, digging down, they reached a layer of compacted earth and debris—of pottery shards, rotted slats of wood, nail fragments, bits of amber glass and two wafer thin bronze coins, of late medieval vintage. Below that, they came upon a circular pattern of collapsed stone, which they had to clear away before finally discovering, at yet an even lower layer, and under a swaddling of linen, the boney remains of a man.

Some kind of dandy, his skeleton was still dressed in a rather fanciful but disintegrating outfit of renaissance vintage that consisted of a velvet jerkin and vest and pantaloons, his boots rotted. Around one of his fingers dangled a gold ring with a cameo onyx setting, bearing, in fact, the stamp of a prominent family. And yes, another detail: his skull was missing. And while such discoveries never particularly surprised Mercado—for before modern times bodies were commonly dumped into wells to poison the local water supply to drive away the local population, or in lieu of proper cremations or burials, during periods of the plague and war—it still seemed a rarity to find the skeleton of a beheaded man. But Mercado, having a memory for some of the most disparate things, immediately thought of something he had once seen on display in the dark corner of a museum in Siena: a fine furlined cap, of the same velvet fabric, atop a yellowed skull, whose forehead had been branded with the symbol of a cross. Found in a buried box found near Orvieto, sometime in the 1870s, a note, written on a piece of vellum, had been stuffed inside the jaw; it read, *"This is the fate of cuckolds."*

A few weeks later, in the kind of intuition that archeologists share with antiquarians, Mercado drove to that museum, and traipsing about its dark and myriad hallways, found the cap and skull—a gristly sight as he recalled—still on display in a dusty cabinet of a room otherwise dedicated to death masks from the plague years and the relics of saints. Sometime later, a forensic anthropologist, with the museum's blessings, examining both skeleton and skull, verified that belonged to the same unfortunate departed soul. Thanks to the ring, those remains were given an identity, that of a member of the noble Colonna clan of Siena, a victim of a vengeful (very pissed off) husband, who had not only cut off his head, but had taken the trouble to dump the corpse into that well, a hundred miles away, four centuries before. The kicker? In helping to solve an old mystery, his simple act of recall had brought Mercado, a minor, if fleeting, moment of celebrity, in the Italian newspapers at least, who printing photographs of his face, referred to him as a "modern Sherlock Holmes of archeology." Going out over the wires, stateside mystery clubs and archeological symposiums asked him to lecture on his find—some even paying him a modest honorarium.

And yet, whenever Mercado went roaming across a meadow, always aware that the earth beneath him in all likelihood could yield something remarkable, he knew well that his archeological life had not

> been spectacular; that he was just a journeyman, at best, whose greatest inward wish had been, beyond all things, to live up to the dreams he once had for himself.

It has often occurred to me since Oscar's death that I too have an "archaeological" life, although it hasn't taken the form that the adjective commonly suggests. I have ruminated on our experiences and travels; I have waded through hundreds upon hundreds—thousands really—of my husband's writings, notes, diaries, correspondence, photos, books, drawings, and collections; I have engaged in conversations about him with friends of old (pals in his orbit before he and I met), mutual acquaintances, and sometimes admirers and readers of his work whom I do not know at all; and I have meditated and prayed in ways that are familiar as well as new and mysterious to me. I had not anticipated that I would have this kind of painfully creative journey at this juncture in my life. It happened as a matter of course, without warning, and eventually led to a need to understand what my existence with Oscar meant while we were together and what it means today. I have dug deep. I have discovered terrain I did not know existed in me.

For most of my life, I was content to exist behind the scenes, working to promote the efforts of those I thought more talented than I, foremost Oscar. (I had not truly cared about acknowledgment for my writing efforts or the work to which I had committed: helping teenagers, especially Latino youth, understand their lives. I was content, always, just to do the work. And I believed that if it was good enough my output would find its way to my intended audience.) This is why I became Oscar's invisible protector. Invisible not only to the public, but to friends and acquaintances in various circles. So unknown was I to some that the husband of a close writer acquaintance, both of whom we saw often, once asked me, "Do you do anything, Lori?"

Behind the scenes of Oscar's public life was my steady involvement. In addition to writing my own books, I read his pages and commented on them almost every day. I took this responsibility very seriously.

Writers know that when they are fashioning a book in its early and mid-stages, it is wise to get feedback from the right people. In the parlance of publishing, it is important to have *a* first reader. Not just any reader but someone whom the writer can trust for his taste, discernment, and accuracy of narrative judgment. It is not easy to find such a person. I suppose in much the same way that an exceptional physician can diagnose a rare medical issue correctly, so too does a first reader see, interpret, and understand the creative flow and intention of a writer's output as it is unfolding mysteriously in the dark.

Oscar and I were each other's first reader once we were married. This arrangement was akin to our sitting on a seesaw.

I went about the task in this manner: I read whatever pages Oscar might give me with enthusiasm and cheerleading rah. No matter what I might have thought, I usually found a way to say that he "should keep going." I felt a responsibility, I suppose, to make sure that he felt confident enough to push ahead. He needed my total support and enthusiasm. So, when Oscar shared his work with me it was with the intention that I would always affirm what he had written. I knew that there would be ample time to make suggestions once he waded deep into his book. In the end, he was a master, and I was very careful about my comments. I had learned that he could become easily riled if I was half-hearted about something that might have been a tad off-key.

Oscar, on the other hand, was a vigorous editor regarding whatever I was writing. By the time he returned any pages I might give him, I could barely see what I had typed. His questions, suggestions, edits, and thoughts were all over the print. So sharp and insightful were his queries that I would usually start over the next day, creating a second draft informed by his close reading. Oscar was, essentially, a dynamo and his engagement with writing was on a kinetic scale.

Other activities I undertook to help Oscar professionally included searching for ancillary materials that might help him in his research. I went on countless library jaunts to seek out volumes that related to the subjects he needed to learn to write wisely about them. I arranged his schedules and mine. I acted as travel agent, first reader, copy editor, translator, counselor, publicist, cheerleader, advocate, go-between, housekeeper, and party planner.

I was also a noise investigator. It happened that any kind of noise, even the whirring of an air conditioner, could be a problem for Oscar. This auditory sensitivity was unique to his personality, and the condition affected us both in different ways. If, for instance, there was ambient noise coming from a closed window in our apartment—a repair being made to a broken water pipe in the street or the sounds of cars racing up the Hudson Parkway—it could throw him, make him truly irritable. Such noise—even hushed noise that he didn't want to hear—could set him off to such a degree that he would find it hard to work or think. He would become rattled. And this would make me anxious. Somehow Oscar thought that I could or should fix any problem that might upset his routine.

I was always trying to figure out ways to reduce or eliminate noise around us. I was a noise detective when we were traveling especially, getting up earlier than him to wander around our temporary lodgings—whether hotel suite, apartment, or vacation house—to determine if there was offensive ticking, drilling, buzzing, or droning. This way I could locate the perfect spot for him to write before he started to notice the dreaded clang or drip, drip, drip.

I have learned that I am stronger than I thought I was and at the same time I am aware that I am more fragile than I ever imagined. But I realize that even in the depths of grief I am persistent in my faith. I have wept bitter tears of mourning while pushing myself to meet the relentless and numbing demands and bureaucracy of American business life.

The ferocity of my mourning has taken a toll on me. In some ways it has broken me. It has been gnawing and ever-present. But I am also faced with another truth: My experience of loss has nudged my heart to think about subjects and persons I could not understand well or know in depth before Oscar's passing. In short, I am more compassionate, more in tune with others' heartache, devastation, and collapse.

Oscar has also revealed himself to me in ways that are unexpected and mysterious, mainly through his fictional protagonists. Now, when I reread one of his novels like *A Simple Habana Melody*, *Empress of the Splendid Season*, or *Blue Antiquity* I see that Oscar is boldly identifying his passions, worries, and interests. For example, take this confession about collecting comic books and how it relates to Mercado's childhood...or should I say Oscar's childhood:

> ...for all the years that Mercado had dropped by that shop, theirs had been an understated way of getting along; for Mercado had long since abandoned any efforts at overt friendship, while the book seller had always seemed content (or let us say as serene as a sphinx) to remain inside his shell. Along the way, Giovanni had somehow managed to survive financially, despite the fact that Mercado had never seen a single other customer in that place. For that reason alone, Mercado, quietly looking around, had always made it a point to buy something from the man.
>
> *"Posso?"* he'd always ask the gent, while picking up some book.
>
> When he had first stumbled upon that shop more than twenty-five years before, while roaming the neighborhood, in that glorious period of happily discovering Rome, he had mainly looked for any tomes relating to ancient history and archeology. If he remembered his first purchase correctly, it had

been of *A Manual of Christian Archeology,* by Orazio Marucchi, which Mercado still owned to that day. (A somewhat somber reference guide to early Christian martyr tombs and their inscriptions, it remained among the books in his study at his home in upstate New York.) He had also picked up several ornate souvenir folios about Pompeii and Rome, the sort that, bound by gold cord, had rice paper between the black and white photograph pages and which tourists would have purchased for a few lire back in the days of Mussolini. Sometime later, as a junkie for all things Italian, he'd bought a turn-of-the-century star-atlas, an issue of Italian *Playboy*, and a scratchy (but did he care?) 78 rpm recording of *Biancaneve e i Setti Nani*—or *Snow White and the Seven Dwarfs*, which held some childhood fairy tale appeal to him; and yes, among other items, during a rainy afternoon, a *Topolino* pop-up book from the 1930s, on whose last page Mickey Mouse signed off with the fascist salute and slogan, "*Sempre avanti!*"—"*To the future we march!*"—a little piece of Italian history. Altogether, they were the sort of things which he no longer had any use for, but had kept, to populate his lonely world, just the same.

And yet, if the truth be told, the overwhelming reason he went into that shop over the years, came down to its fantastic abundance of *fumetti,* or comics, boxes and boxes of everything from Popeye, to Dylan Dog and Flash Gordon, Buck Rogers, Tarzan, Peanuts—(or "*Linus*" as the strip was known there)—and many others, filling the shelves and jamming the floors in dusty cartons. These had always enchanted him. After all Mercado had drawn since childhood and had dabbled with graphic art while in college, a skill that had helped him on archeological digs. But there was another reason: growing up in a household without books, for which he'd always had to fend for himself, comics, from Superman to Bugs Bunny, the sort tossed out by tenants in his building, had been the bread and butter of his first reading, and one of his salvations. In any event, going into that shop, to peruse the shelves, had always been something of a time out from his more serious ponderings, an opportunity to spend a half an hour or so losing himself in one of the more harmless diversions of his past.

Among his favorites and universally popular in Italy, were those editions of *Paperino* and *Paperone di Paperino*, in varying sizes and formats, and from as far back as 1946, that he had started to collect during his first stays in Rome, as a kind of intellectual comfort food—and to pick up on the everyday Italian slang the caption writers used. Known in the states as Donald Duck and Uncle Scrooge, the tales of these orange-billed creatures, always undergoing fantastic adventures, so fit in with the sunnier side of the Italian national character that, years back, it was not unusual for Mercado to come across the most refined, dapperly dressed Antonio Banderas–(or if you like Marcello Mastroianni–) handsome Italian bankers reading such books at lunch in some fancy restaurant or *trattoria* with the intensity of students cramming for a physics exam. Of course, that had all changed—those books having long since been replaced by electronic devices as everyday diversions—a pity, as far as Mercado was concerned. Still, when it came to those duck stories, he was not alone in his interest: several of his archeological colleagues, in fact, were also aficionados of

> those comics, if not for themselves, then for their children. On several excavations over the years he had swapped copies of his Italian duck comics with the archeologist in charge, who, after a day spent in the dusty trenches, had simply liked to read them in the middle of the night, this particular archeologist's favorite tale, it figured, involving a pith-helmeted excavator, set, as he told Mercado, in Ancient Persia. (He once told Mercado that the same story had set him to dream about archeology as a child. But then so many of those stories, as penned and drawn by renowned Disney artist Carl Barks, well-loved in Italy, often involved hunts for hidden cities and lost treasures.) Once, at the Villa *Settefinestre*, while mucking about the Amalfi Coast, near the grand temple site of Paestum, where the Vergilian Society kept a house for fellow archeological travelers, amid its eruditely stocked book shelves, and tucked between the Ovid Review and several volumes on the excavations of Cosa, by the much venerated Frank L Brown, Mercado had been delighted to find a half dozen thumbed over copies of *Paperone di Paperino* awaiting his delectation, the where and how of how they had gotten there a mystery.

Oscar took me to this very shop on our first visit to Rome together and then on every trip to the Eternal City thereafter. I knew that he was introducing me to this store and this gentleman because he wanted me to understand something about his inner life, particularly the fact that he felt connected to some special place within his soul when he was in locales that made him feel nostalgic. Oscar loved discovering comic books and adding to his huge collection of Donald Duck volumes as well as other childhood favorite characters. And this shop surely brought forth many good, old memories of Oscar's early, brilliant days as a fellow at the Academy. He could spend hours, if I had encouraged him, inside that store. But I always got the feeling on those little escapades that what Oscar was trying to recapture was elusive. And that no matter how hard he tried to experience what he had originally felt there...he couldn't. Brazilians have a word for this: "saudade." It is for this reason that while I indulged his habit of making that pilgrimage, I didn't want him to spend too much time there. Inevitably, he would leave feeling a bit let down. And, so, I would suggest a walk in the sprawling Villa Doria Pamphili gardens nearby, which always proved to be a tonic.

Winter Weather

I HAVEN'T BEEN TO FIRST CHURCH in a while. The winter weather has been insistently and unusually harsh the past few weeks, so I have thought better of navigating icy roads. But because there has been a break in the cold, I got into the car and drove the short distance from my mother's house to my library niche to write this morning.

I am hurting deep inside. I am half of a union now. I don't even know what it means to be half of a union. I try not to think about the moment when I learned of Oscar's passing on Columbus Day, 2013, and the agonizing months that followed. But these memories are strong; they keep attacking me. I recognize these remembrances as bullies, enemies. If anyone thinks there is a standard, calm, and systematic way to overcome the knife-cutting trauma of losing your beloved spouse in a flash—of a massive heart attack—on a beautiful, perfectly sunny day in October when everything should be just fine…I don't think that person is really in touch with their heart. The loss of Oscar was and is still unimaginable to me—an all-out assault on my entire being. Simply put, his death was a savage blow to my understanding of reality. And the loneliness that I felt because of it inhabits me still. It's not unusual for me to limp along some days without direction. Lost in thought.

I have pain that I never thought possible. The grief is so profound that, at times, I am a pool of nothing. Yet I am trying with all my might to find my old self. I miss that person, too.

The word most used to explain what should happen to someone after the death of a spouse, child, beloved family member, or friend is: healing. It is an interesting verb for overcoming the tearing away of part of your being. I am not comfortable applying it to what I have experienced, so I prefer the verb *reconstructing*. Reconstruction is what I am encountering.

My faith, which has always accompanied me, is now my life jacket. I pray a lot for strength and for renewed vigor; I know that to be able to accomplish anything worthwhile in the future, I *alone, pretty much,* must find a way to access something of the "old Lori." The Lori who was ever upbeat, joyful, hopeful. Always positive. Steady as can be.

I have begun to analyze this regrettable situation of widowhood. Not just feel it, but truly ponder the condition of being without my husband.

Oscar often wrote about loss in his fiction. In fact, death and immortality are among the subjects that he returned to over and over again in his novels, including *Blue Antiquity*. As I comb this masterful work, I understand the way he circumnavigated the mystery of death. In real life, Oscar would become very quiet when a friend or family member died...as if he was willing himself to disappear. Even a stranger's passing could affect his emotional equilibrium. Any death was reason to mourn for Oscar.

> But during an earlier visit to the eternal city, in the late spring of 2002, when, coming to Rome, he had planned to pursue some research at the Academy library (and to escape the apocalyptic airs of New York and his own sadness over certain matters), it had surprised Mercado, browsing in the shop, to hear the Italian, clearing his throat, ask: *"Tutto bene?"*
>
> "*Cosa*?" Mercado answered with surprise.
>
> "I mean to ask you, *comunque,* how have things been in New York?" he ventured in English. "That's where you are from, where the buildings went down, yes?"
>
> Ah, but the World Trade Center.
>
> "*Cosi, cosi,*" Mercado told him, nodding, with a shrug of his shoulders.
>
> At which point, in a departure from his usual formality, the shop keeper did his best to draw Mercado out on the subject, even gesturing that it was okay for him to smoke one of his MS (*massive stroke*) brand cigarettes if it would make talking about it easier. (He pushed forward his *Cinzano* ashtray on the desk.) If Mercado remembered things correctly about their conversation that afternoon, he'd told the Italian that it had been a very sad and unusual day for him for

many reasons, aside from the general malaise that had fallen over the city; that among the casualties from that disaster were two childhood acquaintances from his old neighborhood in upper Manhattan, "*conosciuta come Harlem*"—or "*'arrleem*" as the Italian pronounced it, repeating that word with savory pleasure. One had worked in a Trade Center rooftop restaurant as a morning sou chef and had been somewhere in that kitchen when the first plane hit, and the other, a janitor or elevator bank operator (Mercado did not recall exactly what he did) had presumably bought his final ticket while getting trapped on one of the middle floors. Not that Mercado had felt particularly close to them, but they'd all attended the same church and grammar school and he'd sometimes seen one or the other hanging around the block when he'd visit his parents—nothing more. But being a few years older and remembering them as young boys, he'd felt their loss just the same.

And he'd probably mentioned to Giovanni that one of his Academy friends, an architect, whom he had known from excavations in Rome, had been riding a train on his way to a WTC plaza restoration meeting in one of the towers at the time of the first impact, those cars stopping dead in the tunnel directly below. (Talk about being rattled; somehow, in the first wave of that disaster, he had gotten out through the darkness to find himself in the midst of the hysteria, the smoke, the sirens above and, some weeks later, had met up with Mercado in a west-side bar, wherein, the two drinking deeply and somehow merrily enough, he conveyed to Mercado the absolutely surreal and terrifying nature of that occurrence, as if—and this was something that Mercado had often heard from anyone even remotely caught up in that tragedy—out of a strange dream.)

The first year of dealing with my husband's death was war. I fought every single day to keep myself afloat. In fact, one morning as I was tearfully sweeping my kitchen floor, I was challenging myself to snap out of my blinding pain, almost fighting with my broom. To focus, to get through the long, excruciating afternoons of silence, I would choose only one activity to tackle—whether going to my lawyer's office for an estate matter or the bank to figure out my finances or the closest supermarket to choose a few items for dinner. Now, more than a decade after Oscar's passing, it is still very hard plowing forward. I ache for him.

It is Spring

IT IS FINALLY SPRING in Chautauqua County, which is a very fine thing to celebrate. The citizens of Jamestown yearn for the budding of April in this remote Southwestern region of the state. They become giddy when the snow and raging winds vanish with the onslaught of daffodils and forsythia. "Spring!" they say over and over, everywhere. But I find myself thinking of Durham, North Carolina this morning and not the flowering crab apple trees and fragile narcissus I saw on the drive to First Church. If ever there were a springtime paradise in the United States, it would have to be ascribed to the splendid, overwhelming bloom of the Triangle: Durham, Raleigh, and Chapel Hill. The outrageous canopy of wisteria, its velvety lavender, wending across the highways and byways of this part of the country in March and April is enthralling. Hundreds of Damson plums punctuate the air. Spring and North Carolina go hand in hand. It was into this beautiful setting that, in 2008, Oscar and I started a new phase of our lives: teaching.

In the spring of that year, Oscar and I began working in the English Department at Duke University, an academic institution that is truly magnificent for its beauty, luxury, aspirational bent, and supremely intelligent student body. The terms of our hire, as put forth by the deans, were such that we were asked to commit to the spring semester each year until we decided to retire. Oscar had been chosen, among a very small and select group of candidates, as a distinguished writer to give heft, cachet, and stardom to the Creative Writing Program, and to ultimately add to Duke's overall stature in ranking. His title was Professor of the Practice. I was hired as a benefit (otherwise known as a trailing spouse) to the same program because of my teaching history (I had taught at three major universities by then) and my publishing record (I had to date produced quite a few books—many anthologies and two novels). I was given the position of Lecturer.

Shortly after Oscar and I accepted the offer from Duke, we went to Rome, as was our custom in September. While we were there, we encountered the Dean of Humanities who was, like us, staying at the American Academy. I remember him saying to Oscar one night, as we strolled down the Janiculum Hill to Trastevere for dinner, "Oscar, we couldn't believe that you accepted the position. We really didn't think you would."

The Dean was right on target. It was a very big leap for us to make because we loved our life as it was: Rome in very late summer and early fall. Residency in

New York City in late fall and winter, and the months between March and June a time for us to travel internationally, which we thoroughly enjoyed, before going to Connecticut for the summer. Oscar made his living from writing—one of a small group of novelists in this country to be able to do so—and he had no interest in teaching at a university. Basically, he accepted the post at Duke because he knew how passionate I was about the job offer and the opportunity to teach, and he was thinking of my well-being and my happiness. Not his own. Our marriage was so seasoned and mature by this time that we truly lived for each other, and in this instance Oscar was putting my desires before his own. I had been deferring to his professional interests over mine for years, and he was completely mindful of this, especially at this stage in our lives. He knew that teaching would give me a lot of joy, and he was acknowledging that he wanted to help bolster my career. It was a time of reevaluation and reassessment of priorities.

Something had happened to our union as the years passed and our tenth anniversary loomed. Instead of cooling, it had gotten stronger, better, and more precious. I can't say that I know exactly why, but my best estimation is this: The literary glamour and hustle of New York City had come to mean less to us. We were searching for more peace and quiet. We wanted to concentrate on producing books for our readers on our terms. Oscar knew that what the critics and system sought to build up and fawn over—namely young, bright, and promising talent, which he had embodied when he won the Pulitzer Prize—was also what they aimed to bring down mightily once that same writer had become established and successful. Sometimes, with delight, I am sorry to say.

Literary society in New York had become the terrain that we had been pulled into in the early days of our romance. There was no getting around it because of Oscar's sudden and overwhelming success with *The Mambo Kings Play Songs of Love.* The receptions, parties, private soirees with extremely wealthy hosts—the titans of New York City industry and commerce—showing off their access to famous artists and the wit and sparkle of their conversation. This world of fetes and black-tie dinners had become commonplace in our lives. Year after year, we duly attended the many invitations that came our way, sometimes as many as four a week. (I certainly helped to keep some fancy boutiques in the black during those years. I was buying gowns and cocktail dresses galore.) And, yes, often we enjoyed these events, but eventually they lost their luster when we figured out what was really going on. The people who handed us their cards with a smile and said, "We have got to get together. Let's have dinner," never did come through. Nor did we reach out to them following amiable chitchat at an art gallery opening or a movie premiere. It was show. All of us strangers aiming to find true friendship on this floating stage that ended up in the middle of an imaginary sea of goodwill. The only common denominator among us was fame. We truly shared very little else.

The nature of literary society in New York City is quite seductive. Once a writer has been admitted to "the club" so to speak, the expectation is that one will participate fully. It often happens like this: A heretofore unknown writer gets a rave review for her first novel from, let's say, a popular radio show host with a lot of clout. Totally out of the blue. (Maybe his best friend read the book and "couldn't put it down, it was so good.") So, the radio host bought the book and read it to find out why his friend was so captivated by it. Suddenly, the aforesaid writer whom no one knows anything about—a total unknown with no track record of any kind in publishing—is on the map. There is a lot of hype. Thousands of people hear the radio host claim that the novel is the "best thing" he has read in years. There are rewards in abundance, now, for the author. The "brilliant" novel makes it to *The New York Times* bestseller list. Money is suddenly flowing—lots of it—not only to the author but to the agent of the author and the publisher. Invitations start pouring in for appearances at receptions, private fundraising dinners, parties, art gallery openings, TV and NPR interviews, and so on. Of course, the writer wishes to be accommodating and helpful to everyone involved, so when the publicist of the publishing house behind this "sudden hit" calls the writer's agent and asks if the newly famous author can be a guest of honor at a very chic dinner party—for a select few of Park Avenue socialites—the author agrees. Then, this happens again. A pattern is established. There are more requests for appearances, more lavish invitations, more opportunities to promote the author's work. More lucre. More fame.

The problem that ensues? For many gifted and promising writers, this world of cozy, privileged adulation becomes the focal point of their lives and not the hard, grueling, struggle of producing the next novel, and the one after that. (I always wondered at these swanky dinners, hosted by truly rich businesspeople, if they understood how hard and unbearably difficult it was to be a successful artist. The chancy quality of it. The unbelievable, mystical thrust of it all.) The work, and the fact that a writer must prove herself over and over in every title sailing forth from her desk, gets lost in this haze of make-believe and beckoning wealth; this hullaballoo is unnatural—even antithetical—to the essence of creating a book. This is why I have always thought that being a writer in New York City is a liability, not an advantage.

There were a few truly painful events—as well as edifying ones—caused by the literary scene. As for the former, I will recount two particularly embarrassing examples, the first more humiliating than the second.

It happened that one day, Oscar received an invitation to be a guest of honor at a dinner in a well-known maven's home on the Upper East Side. It was a charity event of some sort. Oscar accepted the invitation because it was a fundraiser for a cause that mattered to him: education. The dress code was cocktail attire, I remember.

We arrived to an exuberant welcome, with people crowding around Oscar and singing his praises. Within minutes, the hostess took Oscar by the arm and disappeared into the sea of people in the sprawling apartment, leaving me to stand alone in a corner. When this happened (which was often), I roamed around looking at the bookshelves to determine what kind of people our hosts were likely to be. The reception cocktail hour ended, and we were asked to find our dinner seats at the various tables set up throughout the penthouse. Following the beautiful, three-course meal, we were told that there would be music. And sure enough a Cuban band entered the marble-floored foyer and began to play a raucous number. When the hostess came to our table, after the first composition was played, she told us to please get up and "dance for us." Oscar turned bright red, and I turned white, I'm sure. The truth was neither one of us knew how to perform the mambo, although Oscar was a very good dancer, and he could fake it. I could not. She continued, "Show us how a mambo is done the right way." We complied.

When we left the apartment later that evening, we were both so upset by the indignity of having to be "entertainment" for the other guests that we stayed up all night, unable to sleep. That evening bothered us so much that it changed how we decided to attend future "benefits."

The second incident was limited to my discomfort and not Oscar's, although he was involved in an ancillary way. It involved our participation in an annual gala at an exclusive club on Fifth Avenue. I remember exactly what I was wearing, even my choice of jewelry: An Italian, black silk gown and large, gold-drop, pave-cut diamond earrings. Black velvet heels. No purse.

Oscar and I were placed at the same table, which was unusual for these kinds of soirees, but he was sitting across from me. I was seated between two very imposing and formidable businessmen, one of whom was a Wall Street tycoon and the other the owner of a real estate empire. The Wall Street dandy—and he *was* a dandy—began to pepper me with questions about my life with

Oscar, specifically inquiries about how I met him, how long I had been dating him, and why I liked him. Oscar was the evening's guest of honor. I answered my dinner companion with a reserved style. I didn't really think I owed him an explanation about why I "liked" my boyfriend. (I *loved* him.) But the questions he posed became increasingly aggressive, and I started to clam up. I remember taking a sip of wine and swallowing it very slowly before telling him that I would appreciate changing the subject. "Okay," he answered brusquely, "let's dance." The orchestra had begun playing, as dessert was being served by waiters in formal uniform. I looked behind me to see a few couples on the dance floor and turned back to my chocolate mousse. Then, I looked up at him and answered, "Thank you very much, but I'd rather not." To my surprise, my answer infuriated him. The truth was I really did not feel like dancing, but he took my response as an affront and then proceeded to attack me verbally with commentary that I will never forget as long as I live. In a low voice, with hostility, he faced me squarely and spewed, "Why don't you want to dance with me. Really? Because you're with him?" And he flicked his wrist toward darling Oscar, who met my eyes with a smile, not knowing what was transpiring between me and the man to my right. "Wait and see what this novelist brings you in life. Just wait. Everything looks great now. He is riding high, but down the road things will sour with this guy. He's a flavor of the month."

* * *

But there are also extraordinarily blessed opportunities and experiences resulting from literary fame. So many, in fact, that I could write a book about them. I will limit myself to recounting just one: Being sent as a goodwill ambassador abroad by the United States government. This happened several times for us, but I single out our trip to Japan because it was extraordinary.

In 1995 Oscar was asked by administrators at USIA (United States Information Agency) if he would like to travel as an artistic diplomat to Japan and the Philippines. This has been a commonplace practice of our government for decades: selecting high-profile, internationally known American artists to represent our country's global bonhomie around the world. I went with him to Japan, but afterward Oscar flew to the Philippines alone. The experience in Japan is one of the high points of my life for many reasons but chief among them is due to the expansion of my understanding of the multiple dimensions of life; the sojourn in this Asian wonder of a nation changed the way I saw reality. The islands and people of Japan are so profoundly different from our own that it allowed me to grow in ways that I never could have otherwise. Japan is a country that embodies beauty in everything, even the simplest of acts such as sipping a cup of tea. Everything has fundamental energy and underlying meaning...even emptiness. (One learns to look at an empty space and see a thing of wonderment. Its shape, scent, and aura.)

Our trip began in Tokyo and ended there but in between we went to Fukuoka, Hiroshima, Osaka, Kyoto, Nara, and Sapporo. We traveled by bullet train, jet, and private car. We were transfixed by the sensibility of the people we met, their pulchritude, elegance, poise, dignity, honesty, and honor. We were amazed—truly amazed—by the cleanliness that is everywhere, on subways, in taxis, in public lavatories, on the street. The unusual compositions of ancient gardens of sand, water, stone, and vegetation are etched in my memory to this day. These gardens are abundant and give the land a fairytale quality. And the food! I have never seen pastries and sweets more complex and gorgeous in my life. If a rose window in Chartres Cathedral could be replicated in foodstuff, it would surely have its debut in the confection section of the basement food court in a Japanese department store.

Although we continued to accept invitations to special events, gatherings, literary conventions, and international meetings up until Oscar's death, we had begun to retreat. We had become very private. We focused on what made us happy: each other's passions and interests. We especially concentrated on our writing—the demanding labor of trying to create books that could make a difference somehow, some way, in people's lives—and the artistic friends whom we really appreciated and valued.

When we accepted to teach at Duke, we were unfortunately brought further away geographically and figuratively from these dear friends because we simply had less time to commune, but these individuals truly made our lives snappier, more fulfilling, and blessed.

The years that followed at Duke were interesting, to say the least. But of all the vicissitudes and twists and turns on that gorgeous, complex campus, the essential takeaway for us was how much we adored our students.

The young people who attend Duke are, for the most part, exceptional human beings, and it was thrilling for us to engage with them, learn from them, and grow with them. We were the beneficiaries of their youthful optimism, energy, and devotion.

To put it another way, the last days of our marriage were affected by Duke University in ways that no one could have anticipated. Neither the university community nor us. Our lives on that gorgeous campus brought us closer and closer together so that there was no seam between Oscar and me by the time of Oscar's untimely and tragic death. We were simply one cloth.

Privacy and Respect

THE SANCTITY OF OSCAR's and my daily routine was one of the things I held most dear about our marriage. In all the years that we were together, I never once stepped foot into his writing studio. This was his request. I completely understood that Oscar needed that space for himself and for his peace of mind. He was equally respectful of me.

In fact, after my husband passed away, it took me eight years to unlock his office and step inside, such was my gut feeling that to do otherwise would be trespassing. Similarly, when a lawyer friend of mine urged me to find a way to get into his computers to ascertain if there was anything I should see, I declined. I haven't "cracked" his Hewlett-Packards to this day, and I never will.

This respect for each other's space extended to other dimensions of our existence. Rarely, for instance, did I interrupt Oscar's reveries, whether I happened upon him in Riverside Park as he meditated on a bench or saw him from a distance on the street as he greeted an old friend. In the evening, at supper, I rarely, if ever, asked him what he had accomplished that day. I didn't need to; he would hand me the pages he had written and ask me to look at them. And my belief was that if he wanted to confide something important, he would.

While we were matter-of-fact about each other's privacy, there was, however, an aspect of our marriage that might be considered over-the-top: We were exceedingly mindful of each other's safety. We worried all the time about "something happening" to each other.

A typical conversation in this vein went like this. Oscar might come upstairs from his studio to our co-op apartment on a higher floor to search for a book or get a pair of glasses and then ask if I needed anything from the store. I would always say the same thing: "Thanks Oscar, but I'm going to the corner a little later, so no need to worry." His response inevitably would be, "Why do you need to go out, Pupsie?" And I would always reply, "Because we need milk. I need to buy some things for dinner tonight." He would scrunch up his face and say, "Nooooo. Stay in. I'll go instead." And then I would counter, "Oscar, why the worry? What's wrong with me going to Fairway?" His face, a map of concern, would rattle my heart. "What if something happens to you? Someone could hurt you. Something could happen," he argued.

There was an additional worry for me: Oscar's health. From the start of our romance, Oscar had told me something startling and upsetting when we were having dinner in one of our favorite Italian restaurants on the Upper West Side, just before Thanksgiving. Our light conversation turned serious just as we were served our entrees. The subject of marriage had arisen, and we were trying to figure out where each one of us stood on the matter. I truly had not been concerned about marriage; there was something in me from young adulthood that allowed me to entertain the possibility of happiness without ever being a wife. I might not have acted like a feminist overtly or labeled myself as one, but I was an independent-minded woman who aligned herself with a lot of feminist ideology. Oscar was like me in that he didn't care too much about tying the knot. Since he had experienced a disappointing first marriage in his twenties—that lasted just a few months—he wasn't in any rush to try matrimony again. Still, I wasn't *against* marriage. And neither was he. So, when he said, rather abruptly, that he could never get married, he got my attention. "Why?" I asked.

"Well, it wouldn't make sense for me to get married," he answered, "considering that all the doctors have told me that I won't live past my mid-forties." Oscar, at the time, was thirty-nine.

I went silent, my heart falling to the floor. I was trying to think about my response following this heavy, terrible admission. I paused for a few seconds and took his hand. "You mean the nephritis? But I thought it was something that happened in your childhood. You got over that. Right?"

"Yes. But the fact that it was such a severe case, that I have only one working kidney and some other things, makes it likely that I won't live long."

Rather than cry, even though I wanted to, I became stoic, which is my instinctive response when faced with sudden, unhappy circumstances. And then I looked at Oscar and said with a very knowing tone, "Well, I think these doctors are wrong. It wouldn't be the first time that a physician made an inaccurate call. Doctors are not infallible, even though some might act as if they are." Oscar smiled. And we changed the subject to our Thanksgiving plans and our intention to walk around that night looking at the huge balloon figures that were being prepared for the Macy's Parade lined up just a few blocks away from our dining establishment near The Museum of Natural History.

* * *

Nevertheless, I couldn't quite rid myself, ever again, of the nagging thought that Oscar might die before he reached the normal life expectancy of an American male.

When I came upon the following rumination in *Blue Antiquity*, in the years after my husband did die of a massive heart attack, I knew that he had been thinking, as he was writing this excerpt, exactly what his protagonist Mercado was pondering:

> In the darkness, then, with the courtyard sounding with footsteps and voices, and against the backdrop of sprinkling fountain water, it occurred to Mercado that even if he were to go in a year, he would have outlived Jesus by almost twenty-five; Alexander the Great, the same, for they had died at thirty-three, the age at which he had first come to the Academy. He had odd notions just then: of Julius Caesar crucifying ten

thousand pirates along the cliffs of the Mediterranean as one of his first acts as proconsul, each of those men having suffered the same agonies of Jesus, but multiplied by the thousands; that Pericles had rotted from the plague in Athens; and that poor Hunt, who, having possessed a world of knowledge in his head, had been barely even able to remember anything about his life of archeology toward the end, while Cyrus, on the other hand, the King of the Persians, had a memory so good that even in his advancing years he still knew the names of every soldier in his army.

And he dwelled upon all the places he had once dreamed about visiting that he would probably never see: from the temple districts of Angkor Wat to the distant Mariana Islands, to Tasmania and New Zealand, South America, Cuba (that which he had always badly wanted to see), and, as well, the frozen north; or for that matter, the American west, home of cowboys, pueblo ruins and the Grand Canyon, where, on a remote cattle ranch in Wyoming, his old friend Maximilian Gabor had, at the behest of a movie star who fancied himself a living emperor, built an exact replica of Horace's Villa, after the one in the Sabine Hills outside Rome, a place that he had always beckoned Mercado to visit. Perhaps, such thoughts had come to him out a simple craving for *continuing* adventures (and in the spirit of a *Paperone di Paperino* comic, a copy of which he kept by his side)—or simply because, as he lay on his bed, the academy fountain's waters went on trickling, his clock ticking closer toward midnight.

Space

My mother recently returned from Florida where she was vacationing at my sister's home on the Gulf of Mexico. One of the first things she asked me was, "Did you go to the church to write, or did you stay at home?" She presumed, I think, that I would find her absence and quiet in the house sufficient for me to work there. I answered, "Oh, I went to First Lutheran. I need to be there to write this book." She looked surprised but she needn't have been. Writers require *their space*, a specifically chosen place in which to feel connected to their creative source. (I know that some writers elect to write with lots of chatter and people around them, such as the ambience of a Starbucks shop. I have never been one of those individuals; I must be alone. Although sometimes I find that music, played softly, is welcome.)

Writers' spaces are endless catalysts for speculation and curiosity. Fans of certain authors want to know about the environs of the writer whose work they love. Readers flock to the famed residences of greats such as Hemingway, Dickens, Twain, Faulkner, and many others. They need this pilgrimage experience to fully honor the literary work that holds pride of place on their bookshelves and, also, changes their lives in profound and untold ways. Oscar and I were no different, in fact.

I remember that once, on a trip to Madrid, we were staying in a hotel in the so-called Barrio de Poetas, which is an enclave where some of Spain's greatest seventeenth-century Golden Age poets and playwrights lived and wrote. It's on a hill, not too far from Parque Retiro and the magnificent Prado Museum. Very near to where we were staying was the great Lope de Vega's house, now a museum. I was so excited about the proximity of his home to our hotel that it was first on my list of touristic things to do once Oscar's newspaper interviews and promotional appearances were over.

I had been working on the first draft of my third novel, *A Stitch in Air*, at the time and the character of Lope de Vega had inspired a figure very much like him in my story. I couldn't wait to find out if what I had imagined him to be like in his tastes and proclivities would bear out in concrete objects and decor in his private life and home. How would his desk be fashioned, I wondered. Would there be interesting bibelots in his salon? Would I see some of the books he himself read for inspiration? I wanted to know if there was a garden for him to gaze upon from his study window.

I was not disappointed. Lope de Vega's home was just as I had anticipated: richly appointed, full of light, and... yes, there was a garden.

The alluring, walled city of Avila is not too far from Madrid by train, and so we decided to travel there, on the same trip, to see the convent where sixteenth-century mystic poet-nun extraordinaire, Teresa de Avila, lived and worked most of her life. Similarly, I was thrilled to walk through her white-walled, tiled-floored conventual quarters and examine her personal effects. When I came upon a pair of castanets that she often played—according to the explanatory note beside them—I laughed out loud because in my novel Adela, the nun who was modeled after Teresa, played the castanets too. I had made an imaginative connection that was true without ever coming upon this fact in my research.

Admirers of my husband's novels might be asking at this point if I intend to describe my husband's studio—but his primary writing space in New York City is a room that I never saw, as I have indicated. I did have filmmakers go into his study, however, and film it exactly as it was on the day he died. (I have yet to see this footage, but someday I hope to find the strength and courage to do so.) My familiarity with both his studio in Connecticut and the one in our Durham, North Carolina house is a different matter. Owing to the fact that his Connecticut office was so pleasing and comforting to him, and also because I decorated every inch of it, I will share the particulars as faithfully as I can.

The first thing I should say is that our "KP" or, more accurately, Killam's Point abode in the old Connecticut town of Branford was an unusual configuration. It was two apartments, which we rented, on different floors in a brick and clapboard Victorian mansion perched a few feet from the Long Island Sound. We occupied the attic apartment (with a view of the water so breathtaking that at times I couldn't leave my sitting room chair) and a first level, accommodating terraced studio with an extra room for housing Oscar's daily purchases of books, comics, vintage lead soldiers, computers, and office equipment. Oscar's many purchases were made online via eBay or Amazon as well as in the local Walmart, which was hidden behind a little hill in accordance with the community's aversion to big chain stores. But Walmart was one of Oscar's favorite outings on our Connecticut stays. He loved going there. It was the size of the store that intrigued him and the range and abundance of so many items available for purchase. Every other day, Oscar entreated me with, "Hey, Pupsie, can we go to Walmart?"

"Sure!" I always understood Oscar's interest in the store as a *city-boy thing*, as Oscar in his youth hadn't known the suburban habit of "going to the mall" for diversion.

Our first-floor apartment at Killam's Point was Oscar's writing space, and the attic atelier was mine. I made our meals in Oscar's studio kitchen, but we slept in the attic apartment because it had a very nice, air-conditioned bedroom.

Oscar's writing niche blended with the terrain around us; it was all of one piece. Lovely French doors at the far end of the long, sunny room were open fully when he worked, so that he could hear his favorite birdsong and the waves crashing against the private beach just a couple of feet away. Even though Oscar was sensitive to "noise" this kind of natural sound had a very pleasing effect on him: it was soothing, inspiring. The twittering of birds was a welcome melody; the murmuring of the sea was calming. In other words, nature's lullabies were the best kind of sound. Oscar often played music, mainly classical, while he wrote. Music could *never* be noise for Oscar.

Oscar's desk was a simple, old maple table, planted inches away from the French doors, facing the open sea and the little islands in the bay. It looked like the southern coast of Ireland.

I had chosen fabrics for the made-to-order sofa and chairs that echoed the changing colors of the tide: sea green, turquoise, gilt, and gray. The sheer ivory curtains billowed with the breeze that kept the studio at a perfect temperature. The bookshelves, end tables, lamps, and other pieces were antiques that we had found at quaint shops, yard sales, and secondhand stores along the Connecticut coast.

It was a beautiful, comforting space that Oscar adored. He also took pride in keeping it immaculate, especially the kitchen area. I well remember the day he decided to test my observation skills as they related to the area where I cooked each night. Being a tease, he began his challenge to me this way:

"Lor, take a good look around the kitchen."

"Okay."

"Do you see anything different?"

I looked up and down and from left to right. I homed in on the counterspace. I looked at the shelves holding plates and flatware. Bowls. Pans. I examined the oven, the refrigerator door, the sink. "No. I don't see anything different."

"Look again," Oscar instructed. "Look very closely at everything."

"Alright." And I smiled at Oscar with, I imagine, some confusion. Again, I peered at everything around me.

Oscar began to laugh hysterically. "I knew it. I just knew that you would not see what I did."

"Why? Why do you say that?"

"Look above you, Pupsie."

Above me was a rack which held special frying pans. But did I see anything unusual? No.

"Look directly above your head."

Now, I could see that Oscar had scrubbed and polished my favorite nonstick frying pan. It gleamed. In fact, I could almost see my face in the base.

"That's what I did all morning, Pupsie bear." He grinned from ear to ear.

"I see. Thank you, honey!"

"Don't call me honey. You know I don't like that word."

"I meant, Spugsie." The nickname he preferred for himself.

He grinned.

At the end of the day, he played a game of tennis, swam (he had the most elegant crawl of any nonprofessional swimmer I have ever seen, and all of us at Killam's Point loved to watch him as he cut through the waves in our bay), or simply relaxed on the terrace where I joined him to chat with our neighbors—a mix of artists, athletes,

Yale professors, entrepreneurs, and environmentalists. He also made friends with a darling, very precocious little boy named Tim. Oscar adored this child and happily engaged in water gun matches with him for hours.

The folks on our little piece of Connecticut paradise were the best-hearted people we could have ever hoped for as neighbors.

We loved KP, which came to us by way of our cherished friends, Lyda Aponte de Zacklin and Ralph Zacklin, former United Nations diplomats of distinction. We loved the community of Branford so much that I chose the town to be his final resting place. He is buried in a cemetery that abuts the Connecticut River, under a gracious tree.

I will miss our life there until the day I die.

Conversation

One evening, at a reception following a reading Oscar had given at a museum in Dallas, Texas, a well-heeled, very attractive woman approached me and said, "So, you're the lucky one." She had an engaging way about her, and I could tell she wanted to chat a bit. She was curious about what life was like with Oscar. "I just can't imagine how wonderful it must be to live with such a witty, funny, and articulate man!" she gushed. "All my husband does is talk business. And football."

"Well, there certainly is never a dull moment," I replied, smiling back. "Oscar is never at a loss for words. I don't think there is a soul on earth who is like my husband. He is too complex and unusual."

"Oh, I can see that; he is marvelous. I think he is a genius."

This kind of comment was made often by his fans and admirers wherever we went. Men and women alike were always telling me how much they admired him. "What a fantastic guy!" was the usual summation voiced by the men.

And "adorable" was the adjective used most often by the ladies.

Because both of us were reading constantly and writing just as much, which means that during the day we were alone and silent but in the same building—not in a conversational office setting or around colleagues as most workers are—we treasured our dinners together and the evening hours when we could talk...and talk. Our conversations could be spirited, sometimes eye-opening. A typical dialogue could start like this: "Oscar, what did you think of Richard's comment last night? Taking your students to the Met to appreciate just *one* painting on the visit. What a wonderful way to teach how *to see and understand*, right? I love the clapping too. Having everyone stand there and clap for the master."

"Yeah, very cool. Richard is a cool cat."

"So, if you were to take one of your classes to the Met to see just one painting, which work would you choose?"

Oscar might rub his chin. Smile. And then offer, "Velázquez's *Portrait of Juan de Pareja*."

"Good pick. I love that painting; I really, really love that painting. What is it about the visage?"

"You can see his soul."

"Yes. You're right."

"He embodies dignity and light, and Velázquez could capture that in paint. It's genius. An incomparable portrait."

"So, what is genius, do you think? I mean you and I know several brilliant painters, but do they have that kind of talent?"

"Look, there are fine painters in the world. But..."

(Oscar *did love* the work of Stephen Hannock, I know this for certain.)

"Yeah, I think I know where you are going."

"Same thing with writers. I think Borges was a genius, though."

"Yes. Absolutely, but why?"

"I don't think it's possible to put into words. You just know. Maybe because you sense a work's otherworldly emanation."

And so on. We could ramble for hours like this, exploring each other's minds. Sometimes we came upon an impasse but just as often we discovered something about each other that we never knew before. It was fun, serious, and bonding.

We relished lectures at the American Academy in Rome or the American Academy venue in New York City, readings and concerts, forums with writers, musicians, classicists, artists, archaeologists, architects, historians everywhere and anywhere—at The American Academy of Arts and Letters, City College, the New York Public Library, the Museum of Modern Art, Riverside Church, The New School, Lincoln Center, and on and on. We loved to explore each other's reactions to these individuals' knowledge, brilliance, and understanding of the world.

We were always searching to understand what this life "is all about." One of our *cositas*. This preoccupation is so evident to me in the following exchange between Mercado and an elderly gentleman, a regular at a tavola in Rome that both men frequented. It's the kind of conversation, in fact, that Oscar might have had himself with any number of strangers he met in a day:

> At a once dingy *tavola calda* called Bruno's, that he'd often frequented years before it had been turned into an upscale Sicilian restaurant with pastel colored walls, Mercado remembered meeting a burly, bald headed and florid complexioned man, who'd eat his plates of seafood pasta, of small purplish octopi with capers, while drinking down a bottle of wine, sometimes two, until he fell asleep by a smallish cafeteria-style table in the back, oblivious to the world, his face utterly removed from reality as he drifted off into his own memory lane. In a mustardy pin-striped suit that had seen better days, a loosened tie in the tricolors of Italy, and a shirt whose collar he could never fully button around his neck, he'd always seemed reminiscent to Mercado of his superintendent father, Rolando; not just in his burliness, or earthly manners, but for his air of befuddled dissipation.
>
> Late fiftyish looking, the gent often smoked while he ate, a lit cigarette in hand, a fork or a glass of wine in the other, sometimes talking things over with himself. A local character whom the waiters treated with infinite patience, he always struck Mercado as an interesting but lost soul and more than a few times, as he'd struggle to get up on his feet, or went tottering off to the toilet, Mercado felt that he knew him as well as anyone, even if they'd never had the opportunity to speak. But one day, while Mercado had been trying

to explain some overly complicated thing in Italian to the waiter—ah yes, it had something to do with a rumor Mercado had heard from one of the Academy gatekeepers, about a local sharpie, purportedly peddling Etruscan artifacts in that place—this man, sitting nearby, and off in some inward revel, suddenly awakened to intervene. Leaning forward, his veiny head burning, he said to Mercado, in perfectly understandable English, "Forget the Italian, please—what is it that you are trying to explain?"

Well, once he, hearing Mercado out, got around to conveying the young man's somewhat nosy question to the waiter, the tall mustachioed Bruno himself, wouldn't have anything to do with it: *"Niente,"* he muttered, wiping his hands on his long Geppetto apron in disgust. *"No ci sono tombaroli in questo posto,"* with such adamant trembling to his voice, as if to be swearing a pledge over an ancestor's grave. *"Non mai nessuno!"* With nothing more to say on the subject, Bruno went off behind the counter to pound flat some veal fillets with a cleaver, while Mercado, nursing a bottle of wine, which in those days one paid for according to how much one had drank, could not help himself, as the son of Cuban *immigrati,* from asking the man as to how he had acquired his impressive English.

"Oh that," he answered, almost dismissively. "I learned it in the merchant marines, while going all over the world. For ten years," he said. "In fact, I once lived in Brooklyn, in the Red Hook neighborhood, yes indeed, near Bay Street and the Rheingold brewery—do you know it?"

"Of Brooklyn I do," Mercado said, "but not the Rheingold brewery."

"It was in the 1950s, before your time, yes?"

"I was a boy," Mercado told him.

"And me, a very lucky young man. You know, back then I made a beautiful trip, by automobile, across the United States with some friends. We went to the farms of Wisconsin, to Chicago, to the Grand Canyon, and finally to Hollywood, California. You ever been?"

"*Non ho mai stato di la California*," Mercado ventured in Italian. Nor had his father or mother, Mercado remembered thinking. Not to any of those places, for his was a family that had never really gone anywhere outside New York: and there he was, in a *tavola calda,* on a side street in Rome, Italy, drinking wine and frankly getting a little tipsy, and thinking, a little guiltily perhaps, of his own father Rolando, at his age—what was Mercado at the time, thirty four?—and of how much hope his father must have had when first coming to the States from Cuba in his youth; and then, as Mercado sat there so long ago, of his father those years later, a heavy-set man, smelling of boiler rooms and plumber's gum, who, by day's end, had little interest in doing anything more than spending his nights in the kitchen of their fourth floor walkup apartment, eating his meals with abandon, smoking and drinking himself to sleep, as if to forget the world, and the very passing of time; just like this gent seemed intent to do.

"Such nice times they were," he went on. "I was so young and travelling everywhere...."

And he recounted his journeys as a merchant sailor to distant ports and exotic atolls, from Singapore to

Reykjavik, Buenos Aires to Havana, the latter of which particularly caught Mercado's attention—so much envy mixed in with his joy of hearing him going on about his life that afternoon.

Then this man, whose eyes bulged out when he coughed, mentioned that English was but one of the half dozen languages he could speak, that he had enjoyed the carnal favors of women from every country he had visited in those years. But then, as if possessed suddenly by a different kind of spirit, not of amicable braggadocio, but of the sort that makes one turn inwardly, entangled by the caprices of time, he mentioned, as well, that he had once been a priest.

"So what happened, you may want to ask me?" he said, with a shrug of his shoulders. "I don't know. I just got tired of it, that's all. And maybe I lost my faith, who can say?" He puffed at his cigarette, a scent of both tobacco and a lilac aftershave about him.

"But, I can tell you, young man," he went on, "that I really don't have any regrets about my life—over some things maybe—we all do, yes? But what I did I was meant to do."

A bit drunk, he added, while making a sign of the cross in the air: "You know I can still remember the words of the Mass in my sleep, all that '*in nomine Patris, et Filii, et Spiritu Sancti, Amen*', etc., etc., business... Because I will say the entire Mass, from beginning to end without a single pause, I sometimes think that I am still a priest—and that always makes me laugh, for in one moment I am in a whore house and the next kneeling before an altar. As you can see, I am no longer capable of either."

And he took out from his jacket pocket a wadded up brown wallet, dense with slips of paper, from which he retrieved a half-size photograph of himself to show Mercado: it was of a thin, full headed and somewhat handsome priest dressed entirely in black and standing in front of a church, a Bible in hand, a smallish, kindly looking woman by his side.

"This was taken in front of San Lorenzo's *fuori le mura* in 1947. The nice looking lady there is my mother—it's for her that I became a priest." Then, as if to prove that he had indeed been a merchant sailor, he pulled out another card, but laminated, to show him. "Yes sir," he said, with some satisfaction as Mercado looked it over. "I have sailed on every ocean."

Suddenly, in the way that Mercado's father sometimes did at night, he began staring at him, as if trying to memorize his features, his dense fingers pinching at the tips of his inspector Clouseau moustache. Slumping back in his chair and with his eyes closing for a moment, the Italian left the world for a while, until, coming to and focusing intently on Mercado again, he finally got around to remembering that which he had just been on the verge of telling him—a simple homily, or an anti-homily if you like.

"Now listen closely—and carefully young man, for I'm going to tell you something of importance, which I had first heard from my father, and that I will share with you; but in Italian, which you understand, yes?"

"Yes, of course," Mercado answered, a little annoyed.

"It is this—and it will serve you well, no matter what you do, my American friend." And he, of a raspy voice, whispered: "*La vita e bella, ma quando finisce,*

> *finisce,"* the Italian told Mercado. "That is the simple truth, *hai capito?"*
>
> "Yes," Mercado said: "'*This life is beautiful, but once it's over, it's over.*'"
>
> "Bravo," the Italian said. "Now, don't forget it, huh?"
>
> "I won't," Mercado told him.
>
> And now, those years later, while thinking about that heavy gent whose name he may have learned but did not remember, and who in his melancholy reminded him of his father, and for that bit of advice, far more than his own father had ever given him, Mercado obviously hadn't.

Oscar's and my lifelong conversation often related to Oscar's mission as a novelist, although he would surely wince if he heard me call it as such. He was loathe to think high-mindedly about his work and he detested precious language. He thought of himself as a craftsman and stylist, yes. But instead of "mission" he would prefer the word *intention*. He was writing to blow away the dust of dullness and to ignite passion in his readers. There was little he disliked more than a hardened human heart. He wasn't interested in individuals who failed to contemplate history and the lessons it provides. He couldn't understand how so many people could go through life not wanting to know about the Roman Empire, or ancient Greece and the philosophers, artists, and leaders who shaped their world, our world. He had little patience for Americans who weren't curious about the global stage or never bothered to investigate their own family history or their antecedents' circumstances. Why? Because he knew he owed his forebears. That we all owe those who have come before us for struggling, laboring, and suffering to procure a better life for those who have followed. Oscar's preoccupations often became his literary "obsessions." The main themes of his oeuvre were related to familial love, identity, passion, the search for God, and the meaning of death and eternity. I liken the effect of his pen to that of a match lighting paper. It would be very hard for anyone to read an Hijuelos novel and not feel heat.

Take, for example, these pages:

> Oh, but the highlights of those months, interspersed in Mercado's head as he walked around the grounds: first came that daily immersion in the quietude of nature, for Mercado, out in the field, soon discovered that despite his urban orientation to the world, he absolutely loved the countryside's beauty—the pines and olive and fig trees, the fields of wild flowers, of violets and angelica, and the sight of sheep and horses roaming in the distance, of the dreamy miasma floating in the air, of wispy dragonflies and fritillaries drifting around, the perfumed wisteria cascading over lane walls, and of the most incredible bird song, sparrows darting, bouncing daintily on their narrow heels everywhere. In that time, he learned that swallows, turning in wild spirals over the tree tops, loved excavations; and more mundanely, that an orderly room in an excavation house was rare: bathrooms were often a disaster of dirty trousers, socks and t-shirts, and mildewed towels; that mosquitos colonized the light bulbs, dampness being everywhere, that the water sometimes came out brown from the tap; that the post-college age excavators had not yet shorn their

dormitory habits and, in any event, with three to a room, the scant space and dirt and clay that everyone trudged in after the day's work produced a particle and grime-ridden world—that if you shuffled across the tile floors in your bare feet, you had to eventually wipe them clean before putting on a pair of fresh socks, if you had them. Balconies were commonly draped with sink-washed underwear, panties and t-shirts and bras; drains clogged with hair, the mattresses, such as they were, soft and stained with sweat. But, on the other hand, there was the smell of dusk—of pine trees and fields of flowers, meadow bonfires, the chortle of birds, trees that rustled through the aubergine night, and somehow, always from the distance, the scent of fresh-baked bread.

The work itself, involved hours and hours of digging; of getting down on his knees and pulling up thick patches of overgrown vinery, of his hands growing raw and pricked by the thorns, even through a pair of gloves, all the while watching, the sun moving slowly over the treetops the sun, the forest's shadow edging along the trench, and over a well, toward the field. Those years before, he learned that excavations proceeded slowly—he could not think of a single thing from his life back in New York that took or felt so long as some of those days, save perhaps that tedious and somber part of the Mass known as the Offertory, when time slowed, almost to death; or perhaps the monotony of waiting endlessly on a subway platform in the Bronx at two in the morning for a train to finally approach the station. However, though time moved slowly, the natural setting could be quite pleasant onto itself, what with the olive and fig and oak trees breathing softly in the distance, and, on a mild day, the most delicious mimosa rich breezes, with a hint of the salt air and blossoms, blowing in across the meadows from the sea.

And archeologically speaking, the Villa Priscis was indeed one of those sites that over the years kept yielding new artifacts and architectural remains from many an era—from the Etruscan, to the Roman, the Lombard to the Christian, the exquisiteness of which at first escaped him; for, back then, the startling apparent incompleteness of it all, dug deep grooves into the fantasies he had weaved beforehand: and the labors—of yielding a pick and shovel in some spot for hours at a time (and hard, so as to impress everyone with the techniques he'd learned working for his older brother) as well as filling up one wheel barrel after the other with dirt and stone and whatever debris he encountered, while building his own little hill of it, became, as the day(s) wore on, a bit more grueling than he had counted on. Thankfully, Hunt spelled him with other tasks, of a less challenging nature—of washing out pot shards (for they found them by the hundreds), combing the mounds for artifacts—for you never know what might be lurking inside that pile of dirt amongst the worms; and, to his greater satisfaction, he indeed had Mercado make some elevation drawings, depicting, as per Hunt's instruction the various levels and kinds of brick in what, for his (and Brown's) purposes, would be ultimately identified as "Anteroom A," Mercado to repeat those tasks, with other rooms, over the years.

Then too, as exciting as finding any Roman *denaro* or a loom weight in the ground, were the females who made the hours pass more easily—oh, to have peered over at some Sardinian or Boston girl, superbly tanned and fit, exposing her scrumptious cleavage while bending forward to dig out some hole, her entirety quivering, and the sight of her sinews, as they rose along her thighs where the edges of her dusty shorts pressed into the inguinal loin. He passed the hours so smitten with one or the other of the young women who came to work at the dig, sometimes for days, that Mercado, putting his more pious proclivities aside and daydreaming about them instead, constantly vied for their attentions.

He'd take his meals of pasta and jug wine with the crew in a stucco- walled candlelit room where they'd pass the evening in excited conversation, about dissertations, future job prospects (or the lack of them), and often enough, in the context of other interesting digs that they aspired to—places like Troy or Sardis or in the Roman forum—all the unwritten history they could look forward to in their nascent careers to deciphering—life, the world, and countless moments of small discoveries awaiting them. And though he got along well enough, with them—youngsters from Princeton, Harvard and Yale—he, so new to such talk, tended to be the quietest one in the room. (What could he have talked about? That his Pop was a superintendent, who drank too much? That just before he left for Italy, his mother had blessed him with Holy Water, followed by this bit she did with her hands, shaking them over his head to drive out any evil thoughts or spirits? Or that he always kept the black rosary his mother had given him for his First Communion in his pocket? Or that he suffered from nightmares, worrying about his father, somehow in those dreams—or memories—always roaming in the basement, forlornly, and drunk, a look upon his face, as if he were going to his doom?)

Nevertheless, despite his quiet ways, he with his drawing skills had been pegged as the crew's artist in residence, as it were: for, after the day's work, and sometimes on break, he'd go off and with a wash of ink and water dash off some rather good drawings on a pad of some feature of the Villa grounds, mainly of the landscape and of picturesque trees, which he often gave away as presents; and though he did not have a lot to say in those days, he smiled readily enough, for indeed, Mercado considered himself a quite lucky fellow. Which is to say, that he always remained good-natured about things, nodding with attentiveness, when Hunt, presiding over the table before going off to bed, held forth about the great progress had been made on a particular day, even when, and it happened often enough, the latest trench they'd dug had led to nothing but a higher piling of dirt. Mainly, about such evenings, Mercado remembered the feeling that he had been let into a brotherhood and sisterhood of some kind, even if only fleetingly so; and, best of all, those years later, the special attentions lavished upon him by an aspiring restoration expert whose name, still unforgettable, was Polly.

* * *

Something about his street smarts, along with his pensive manner, and the way he would sometimes just look off into the distance, as if in a dream, had gotten to her. And it did not hurt his chances that she, a solitary sort herself, had broken off things with some guy in Indiana. He'd learned of this one day while watching her applying a tincture of diluted hydrochloric acid to a piece of faded fresco on a wall. Something about laboring in the quietude of such an isolated place, and the repetitious nature of the tasks, far removed from one's usual context, with history swirling all around, provoked their mutual attraction. At first, at lunch time, they would leave the site and walk along a sheep trail toward a lookout over the sea and sit talking—about what Mercado could no longer remember—but behind some trees they'd kiss and fondle each other, and were it not for the possibility of being discovered, they might well have gone further.

But one night, while everyone else had gone to town, the inevitable happened: a tapping at his door and Polly, a tallish redhead and former swimmer, holding a bottle of grappa, came to join Mercado in his room. Sweat in the damp between her buttocks, her dense and muscular physicality, her wet kisses, the prettiness of her ovular face and blue eyes, the heat of her sun-burned skin above her breasts against his chest. Mercado, at one point, felt smitten with the neutrality of time in such a place, feeling insanely lucky to be looking upon her nakedness, and thinking, as if it were a wildly original thought, "the human body has not changed one bit in a hundred thousand years." Not much noise, much bodily exhilaration, and in his later memories, Polly's face turning into that of a dozen or so others, whom Mercado, over the years, in the excitements and amity that develops in such an archeological setting, would also get to intimately know.

* * *

And that had been the summer when he had the good fortune—and honor—of meeting the much-venerated archeologist, Frank E. Brown, then moving toward the tail end of his distinguished career, among his projects the great excavation at Cosa down the coast. This diminutive and understated gent, a former Intelligence officer and spy for the British in the middle east during WWII, a longtime excavator of a site known as *Dura-Europos*, in Syria, where an intact ancient Roman armory had been uncovered; and a compiler of Cosa's town plan—half a lifetime in the making—had, at the invitation of his old friend Doctor Hunt, come by one afternoon for a late lunch, to which the crew, their duties suspended, had been invited. There, by a long table set out on the veranda of the main house, the youngsters, relishing their break from routine, ate a meal of home-cooked pastas with some veal and lemon on the side, but mainly swilled, in the giddy camaraderie of excavators, quite a bit of good local wine, all the while listening with some captivation to Doctor Brown's tales of his many archeological adventures; the more they sipped, the better they became. Speaking softly, he, a puckish white-haired man, with clear blue-gray eyes, who not once took off his beret and dressed almost entirely in black, nevertheless seemed to hold his much younger audience in thrall—his eyes, lit by intelligence and experience, growing wide as he, when asked if there had ever been a site he had wished to excavate, or of "one that got away"—spoke of a temple of Zoroaster in the Iranian desert, a site whose grandeur and alabaster columns

> he had only briefly glimpsed, and tantalizingly so, in the wake of a sandstorm, and whose location, buried within a day or two after by an even fiercer storm, he, in the thirty or so years since that had passed, could never find again. What else could he do but shrug, and sip his cup of wine, his bemused, stoic, slightly wistful expression, speaking volumes as to what he missed: the tantalizing temple, which he will never enter, whose depths he will never know.
>
> To such youngsters, like Mercado, the story spilled over with the romance of what can only be called the chase, the pursuit of the unknown, the possibilities of solving a mystery, of uncovering some lost traces of the past. Which is to say, that, aside from experiencing the honor of shaking the man's calloused hands that afternoon, he, in such a setting, first felt the caressing touch of archeology, however remote as a possibility for his life, as if it were a beautiful woman, a Daphne, a Demeter, an Aphrodite, shimmering in his soul.

In my estimation it's the little things of familial life that give it a beautiful patina. The private, small rituals that couples are apt to observe to imbue their existence with a sui generis quality.

One of my best friends sometimes regales me with stories about her husband that highlight his faults; faults that get under her skin. I am always amused by these anecdotes. She never discusses his peccadilloes in a bitter way. It's always with mild exasperation. I often laugh when she looks at me so earnestly and recounts the same old complaints. They are little things in my mind. Nothing earth-shattering that could harm her love for him.

And I want to tell her that she should look at these minor infractions as the attributes that make him so endearing. I don't, though. I guess I like to be amused by her tales. I don't want her to stop repeating his habits because they make me like him even more.

It's the quirks about the way spouses treat each other that stamp their marriage. Oscar and I held hands a lot, for instance. It was an unconscious thing. He simply reached for mine; I reached for his...in a cab on the way to a major reading he was to give, let's say, at the 92nd St Y. Or just walking through Riverside Park to the tennis courts where he often played. There were so many *cositas,* or little things.

Every morning the first question Oscar asked me was, "What time is?" I waited to hear this twist of English grammar each day because it was adorable. His native Spanish was present in his sophisticated and masterful English even though he didn't know it. In Spanish the inquiry "Qué hora es?" is literally translated as "What hour is?" The direct object pronoun *it* that follows *is* in English is absent in Spanish. One needs to hear this construction, learning the language from immersion, to know it. I never corrected this little kink in his English because it was just so charming.

Our ritual of going to Oscar's favorite comic book store near Times Square to roam and discover a special issue, followed by his insistence that we buy a couple of hot dogs at Gray's Papaya; playing hooky by rushing off to the Met to look at the Egyptian wing on a really bad day; listening to Bach 24/7 on WQRS during the quiet week before New Year's; watching a beloved film like *Spartacus* for the hundredth time; splurging on a really lavish lunch following a morning of frenzied Christmas shopping at Macy's or Bloomingdale's; or reading aloud to each other from a cherished book and our manuscripts in progress. In fact, reading aloud to each other was a habit that was established very early on, a few weeks after Oscar was interviewed by me at the Center.

After our Books and Breakfast program in 1983, he mentioned that he had begun working on his second novel and he casually asked if I would be willing to come by his apartment to take "a listen."

"I'll read some pages to you," he said smiling. And, so, one day I found myself sitting in a comfortable chair, in Oscar's living room on the Upper West Side, being regaled with gorgeous prose. Oscar sat on his couch and read about ten pages from his work in progress and what I heard was fascinating, a riff about ghosts. (These were pages that would eventually be edited out of *The Mambo Kings Play Songs of Love* by Oscar himself.) At one point during his recitation, he managed to look up at me and say, "I'd really like to bite your neck." He smiled.

I thought, *Oh boy, I've got to be careful with this guy.*

For Oscar and me, reading aloud to each other was a must. We loved to do so whenever we found a literary nugget too good to be consumed alone. Certain stories appearing in newspapers were also shared. I remember once, when Oscar was mulling over a particularly sad account of child abuse in *The New York Times* he cast the following remark toward me, "You won't believe this. You just won't believe this." Then, he chose one particularly jaw-dropping sentence to share, followed by, "How could anyone do that to a child?"

Watching Oscar read to me was wonderful enough because he was open, giving, and joyous in his recitation. His face shone with understanding. But it was his voice that had me spellbound. A deep and mellifluous baritone with just a touch of honey to heighten his register and make it decidedly sweeter than not.

The last book from which Oscar read aloud to me is entitled *Hermits: The Insights of Solitude* by Peter France. It was a book he was reading just before his death. I keep it next to my bed along with my Bible.

There was, also, the need to entertain one another.

And our favorite way of doing this was the "guessing game" we played whenever we were sitting next to a restaurant or café window, which was our seating preference. Oscar would begin our exercise like this:

"So, what is that woman's story?"

"The woman with the purple hair who just walked by?"

"Yeah, that one."

"She just found out that her maudlin aunt Anna is coming to New York City from Puerto Rico, the one who was a nun for thirty years. She can't bear the thought of Anna spending two weeks with her in her studio apartment. This purple-crowned niece has lost it. Went to the CVS, found some hair dye. It's a way to assume a stance of empowerment when Anna steps through her door."

"I think she is an art teacher at Collegiate. She wants to come across as cool with her students. She is feeling great and can't wait for Monday morning."

Then from me, "How about this guy?"

"The young dude with the slicked-back hair, Ray-Bans?"

"Uh-huh. I'd say he is an actor. A Broadway up-and-coming star. He is rushing to the August Wilson Theatre. Rehearsal."

"No. Don't think so. I think he has just left his new girlfriend's apartment on West End. Can't stop smiling because all he can think about is how he can't wait to see her again tonight. He is taking her to Giovanni Venti Cinque. He saw the dress she is going to wear, laid out on a sofa. A navy Armani silk sheath. Very elegant."

"Oscar, how about the woman sitting behind me?"

"She has just returned from a month in Rome. She is sick of pasta. And she is loving that Peking duck and the pork dumplings."

"Hey, let's order some Peking duck. We haven't had it since Marty's Christmas party."

"Whatever you want, Pupsie."

Finally, perhaps the most important of the *cositas* in our lives was celebrating birthdays, especially his. In truth, Oscar loathed the weeks leading up to August 24th. In fact, during the first years of our marriage, I was baffled by his bad mood during this time of year. He became depressed, listless, and angry. This was particularly true of the summer Oscar turned sixty. His yearly malaise was more pronounced than ever and began earlier in the month.

Because I knew Oscar had not experienced the kind of childhood birthday parties many American kids enjoy and expect, I always tried to do something unique to celebrate his special day. He simply hadn't been given the sense that it was a day to be pampered by family, or to enjoy with his friends. He had never known a traditional celebration with lots of games, presents, singing, cake, and ice cream.

I decided to make his sixtieth birthday a day to remember and went about planning all sorts of events that would start in the morning and end at midnight. An extravaganza.

One morning, a month before his birthday, I took out a large sheet of paper and listed all the "presents" that he would receive…starting with his annual peanut butter and grape jelly sandwich and culminating in champagne and cake. I wanted Oscar to experience joy. There were unique adventures and activities he had never tried or participated in, along with his daily swim. I had enlisted my neighbors to help me arrange the various special moments and escapades ahead.

The morning of his birthday, I jumped out of bed and put on a pot of coffee, made his breakfast treat, and grabbed my poster with each activity listed by number. Then, I tiptoed back to our bedroom and woke Oscar up nearly singing, "Today is going to be a unique day. A happy day! Wake up, Oscar!" He looked at me forlornly.

"So," I continued as I unrolled my large, handwritten list in front of him, "here are the offerings of the day. Happy Birthday!" I announced each activity by number. Eight total. "Doesn't it sound like a great day?"

"Grrrr."

"Okay. First, your sandwich."

Oscar slowly got out of bed with a scowl and walked into the sitting room. I had arranged his breakfast tray in front of the window facing the Long Island Sound. The sun was dancing on the waves. A fresh, not-a-cloud-in-the-sky morn. I was beaming.

"Alright, high tide is around the corner, so next a swim in the bay. Okay?"

"I guess. This sandwich tastes good. Thank you, Lori."

The look on his face was heartbreaking, a mix of sadness and humility—way too much humility.

"Now, go downstairs, get your swim gear, and I'll sit on the dock with you."

"Alright."

The next hour was routine. I sat on the large, square float attached to the dock and kept my eye on Oscar as he swam the long way out to the major point of our little island. He always wanted me there, to watch...in case. (I say *in case* because while he never articulated any fear about being in the ocean, I understood that he was worried he might have a serious health event while swimming. He was acutely aware of his father's early death by sudden, catastrophic heart attack. Nothing need be said on Oscar's part. *He knew that I knew why he wanted me there.*)

After his two-mile lap in the bay, he felt better. And he wanted to sit on the float a while and talk about a book he was reading. I could tell that the day was off to a better-than-hoped-for start.

"So," I said, after a half hour or so, "I have some errands to run. I won't be long, but I do need to get a few things from Guilford."

"Guilford? Why are you driving all the way there?" he asked.

"Oh, I found a great Italian cheese shop [fib] and I want to buy a few items for snacking."

"Really? Well, okay. But Pupsie, be careful. That's a long drive."

Oscar went back to his studio to write, and I went to a party shop to pick up sixty technicolor helium balloons to make the hours ahead a little zippy.

I don't know how I managed to get those rambunctious balloons into the car, but I did. And I carried them up the little hill to Oscar as soon as I returned.

"Surprise!" I yelled out as I nearly tripped entering his space.

Oscar, in his writing chair, turned toward me. Seeing my balloon bouquets in each hand, he jumped up to help me. "Wow, Lor, these are great!"

"To brighten your day," I answered. I was feeling happier and happier about Oscar's mood change. My plan was working.

"Okay, Oscar. I'm heading upstairs to do a little work. Remember that Claire is coming by to take you to Bishop's Orchard."

Claire, our lovely neighbor and community leader, had offered to take Oscar blueberry picking. This would be Oscar's first time foraging. And he *loved* blueberries.

Then, after a few hours of that exercise, Claire's daughter, Susan, had offered to take Oscar on a tour of Killam's Point to show him secret spots that only the lifelong residents knew about. Beautiful hidden coves, neat diving places on the cliff facing Johnson's Point, special wildflower patches, and the interior of the nineteenth-century bowling alley that was off-limits to everyone but a few residents. This historic Connecticut landmark was behind the clay tennis courts and served as a warehouse for fishing gear and such.

These little escapades would allow me to pick up Oscar's chocolate mousse cake from the bakery, unheeded. And I needed time to decorate his terrace with special snowflake lights I had found in New Haven. I wanted the night's celebration, with our friends, to be especially festive and atmospheric.

Late in the afternoon, I had arranged for Oscar to have a piñata bash with his little friend, Tim, and a few of the neighbors' grandchildren. (I had bought the piñata and the candies, coins, and figurines within it a week before.)

The piñata hour was a hit with everyone. Oscar laughed and ran around with the kids, hitting the rainbow-colored donkey as if he were a kid himself. He was more joyful than I had seen him in a while. Completely free of worry.

The end of the day arrived, and the two of us went to the best restaurant in the area—Le Petit Café—where the amiable owner/chef, Roy, was awaiting us.

That evening, after we had returned home, I told Oscar that I wanted to accompany him to his studio. I had a little surprise for him. Everyone was waiting on the deck quietly in the dark. When I opened the screen door connecting his writing area to the outside terrace, I turned on the lights that decorated the space and our neighbors shouted in unison, "Surprise! Happy Birthday!" Oscar was beaming. Really beaming. He reached out to everyone and there were many hugs and "Hey, man, thank you"s from my birthday boy. He was showered with meaningful gifts, such as a tide clock and vintage toys. Champagne was poured and scrumptious cake was devoured, old stories were told, and many toasts and tributes were shared, among them a lovely song, a thrilling tribute from a dear Duke colleague, and a poem recited in Spanish. The kids ran around with the helium balloons yelling "Happy Oscar!" A perfect coda to a lovely day.

But, of course, later that night, there were butterfly kisses, another one of our *cositas*, in bed.

Summer

IT IS A VERY HOT END OF SUMMER in my hometown this year. Today is Sunday, and I should be at church… worshipping. But for some reason I'm not motivated. I feel lethargic. The thought of slipping out of my Turkish caftan and into church-appropriate clothing has me daunted. So, I pour another cup of coffee and succumb to inertia.

Ferragosto, as the Italians term the oppressive month of August when heat and humidity are at their worst, is particularly wrenching and upsetting for me, especially since my husband's death. Too many memories.

Oscar's absence has made me painfully aware of the things that were never said but should have been articulated; the acts that never happened but might have happened; the memories that could have been made; the histories that might have been discovered but never will. I think about all the hugs and kisses we might have had before us, the longed-for travels, the enlivening times of museum-going, the incredible conversations. It is a wistful time for me. I am listless. The loneliness I feel is reminiscent of the loneliness described by Mercado after his mother died.

> It may have been coincidental, but when his mother had died, and his life began to feel somewhat lonelier than before, he had abandoned so many of the physical routines that had once kept him fit: a former scamp on the tennis courts of his college, a doubles fiend known for his fearlessness by the net, with a zipping serve, he abruptly lost interest in the game; and when it came to twice weekly mile swims at the local YMCA indoor pool, or his increasingly rare half hour jogs along wooded trails (or for that matter, the long treks he once thought nothing of undertaking through the mountains of Adirondack Park), he had let all of that fall by the wayside, what with only so much time in each day. Instead, save when he had to go down into the city to attend to his father Rolando, or some family affair, he withdrew into a somewhat solitary existence.

Just like Mercado, I find myself imagining scenarios and situations as a backdrop to what I am doing in real time. I can't help myself. Making up these backdrops can be disconcerting and paralyzing. The *what ifs* and *whys* haunt me in August more than in any other month. Today, the traditional day of rest, finds me in a state of daydreaming and thinking endlessly about the past. But I have decided to focus on all the extraordinary traits about my husband that continue to bless my life. The beautiful memories of his spirit are front and center as I focus on what made my husband so very unique.

First, I would say it was Oscar's sweetness and generosity that seemed to catch people by surprise and made them crazy about him. Sweetness of temperament, sweetness of actions, sweetness of words. Who thinks to send his wife's parents a two-pound box of chocolates every month? My generous Oscar. Who meets a struggling writer at a fancy reception and offers to introduce him or her to an esteemed and out-of-reach editor? My caring Oscar. Who watches a young woman wrestling with her rolling suitcases along a cobblestone street in Edinburgh, Scotland, and says to his wife, "She can't handle all that weight. Let's help her." My gentlemanly Oscar. Who buys a kindly waiter a guitar when that waiter shares the fact that he would love to learn how to play but can't afford the instrument? My over-the-top Oscar.

Secondly, there was his ebullient nature. His gusto for everything from a delicious grilled steak dinner at Scarpone in Rome to his enthusiastic offerings to help his buddy, Mark McIntyre, prepare the tennis courts in spring, where he cavorted like a kid in New York City's Riverside Park. My darling Oscar.

Thirdly, his playfulness. Ah, his childlike essence, so evident in his habit of arranging tableaus of his beloved lead figurines and soldiers—anywhere and everywhere—to delight me.

Once, after a particularly challenging and disappointing day, I went to bed to find a parade of prancing, miniature rabbits, a spiffy dog, and a calico kitten upon my pillow. At the head of the procession was a tiny princess and a tiny prince dressed in enameled ermine, all French Mignot figures I think.

I ran to find Oscar sitting in his room. He was beaming to himself.

"Oscar," I crooned, "I love my little parade! It's adorable! It makes me soooo happy!" I grabbed him around his shoulders and planted a kiss on his lips.

"You like it, Pupsie bear?" He was grinning ear to ear.

"I love you, Oscar. I love you with all my heart. Who on earth would think to do such a thing? Only you, my love. Only you."

The truth is that I was, and continue to be, blessed by my late husband's immeasurable and luminous humanity. I am aware of this every day.

Oscar's spiritual presence in my life is more insistently ardent in the month of August. He continues to nurture my stalwart faith. He continues to grow in my heart. And even though my mood has been somewhat desultory today, my soul is leaning toward immense thankfulness for so much kindness and affection directed toward us from thousands of individuals throughout the years. I am counting my blessings, among them the unusual, very particular gifts of vision Oscar shared with me. His ability to see what others could not was uncanny. Sometimes startling. He was endowed with another eye, one that spotted the natural magnificence that most human beings don't notice or fail to register. Here is an example.

Two months before Oscar died, while we were in Connecticut, he came to me in silence and beckoned me to follow him with a wave of his hand. It was dusk, the light of August beginning to fade. He didn't say a word, but I knew he was about to show me something special, something worthy of remembering forever. I left my seat on the terrace and walked with him through the grassy lot next door and around the old barn that held our neighbor's tools and whatnot. On the farthest side of the barn, near a stand of trees and bushes, he stopped and pointed. Again, without saying a word. What was before us? A spider web of gargantuan proportion. A filigreed net that extended from the height of the old wooden barn to the ground. It was as if someone had put up a lacey sheet, maybe seven by seven feet, connecting the clapboards to the trees about five feet away. And there, like a dark black jewel in the center—was the spider herself. I thought that it resembled a mammoth Queen Anne's lace, so similar in look and design was the web to one of my favorite wildflowers. The look on Oscar's face was arresting and indelible in memory; it was a mix of disbelief, appreciation, awe, and humility. His eyes were pure light.

Insomnia

THERE CAN BE A LOT OF "I'm not sleeping" in the life of a writer, and in our writing marriage this lament was no less true. Plain old worry—that miserable human vexation—causes most of the insomnia and, also, the fact—at least for us—that it's hard to turn off the engine of one's imagination when in the thick of writing fiction. A whole world is being produced out of thin air every day. The fire, the energy required to construct a narrative, is all-encompassing and draining. The fabricated characters and situations manufacture a parallel life to the "real" life that the author is navigating daily. The writer, therefore, lives in between these two realities and, also, *in* them simultaneously. Tremendous inner strength is needed to push and expand upon the act of making a fictional world a completely believable one. It is hard to step away, even to sleep.

But getting back to the first reason for restless nights: anxiety. Oscar sometimes admitted to me that he worried we would "end up on the street." This may sound ridiculous to some people given my husband's success, but the truth is that a writer's life—again, just like most artists' lives—is engineered by fancy and the stamina to concretize it. And in a world of hard, cold requirements—paying the bills, obtaining health insurance, keeping a house, balancing a bank account—if you don't succeed with imagining a reality that someone wants to read (and the critics praise to the hilt) where do you get the do-re-mi to meet such demands? This is why so many writers take teaching jobs or jobs in publishing as a safety net.

Individuals who are on a payroll know, for the most part, that on a particular day each month there will be a deposit in their bank account for their labor. Not so for an artist. The anxiety can be overwhelming. *Where will the money come from?*

Sleepless nights ensue. The tossing and turning, getting up and moving around. Watching a movie, listening to music, writing notes, paying bills—these were our sleepless night activities in our Riverside Drive apartment in Manhattan.

And now? Well, these days I am plagued by even more sleepless nights than I endured years ago. There are multiple reasons for this terrible situation. And I say terrible because as I age, I find that not getting sleep has truly damaging effects on my body, spirit, and psyche. If I am unable to rest, in the morning I can barely function.

Perhaps the only positive in this unfortunate state for me is this: my main activity throughout the night is praying. I do not read; I do not watch TV or do anything that I might have done when I was younger except for taking care of bills...the endless bills.

Mostly I pray. My prayers are for greater understanding of my walk with the Lord. I know that my Savior is with me…always. I feel God's presence every day. But I pray that I can truly be aware that the Lord is leading me toward my purpose, *still.* I pray that I can be forgiven for any pain I may cause others, that I can forget any hurt that comes my way, that I can overcome the lack of understanding that exists between me and some of those I love. I pray that Jesus is so bright in my life that all I can see is His protection, His mercy, and His love. I pray that my love can grow for others.

I end these final thoughts with the following from *Blue Antiquity*, a description of faith coming straight from Oscar's inspiring spiritual reserve:

> That other Mercado went to church every Sunday and believed that somewhere inside the altar rested the dormant form of Christ, whom he always imagined could listen in on his every thought. The fact that he actually said prayers aloud by his bed at night, until he was about fourteen or so, provoked his older brother, Manny, a Vietnam vet and jazz musician, who'd played in salsa bands in the Bronx (later a trumpeter in a Fort Apache ensemble) and was something of a ladies man—("pussy hound" in the local vernacular)—to a kind of pity—as in, "When are you finally gonna grow up, brother?" But even such remarks did little more than goad him into closing his door, Mercado remaining certain that he and God were, if anything, striking up an unbreakable, ever enriching bond, as if his soul, as he conceived it, had changed from a spirit inside him, into something akin to an impenetrable suit of armor.

The Radiant Life

LATELY, I HAVE BEGUN ATTENDING the Sunday morning coffee hour at First Lutheran. It is held between the laid-back, folksy 9 o'clock service and the formal, more liturgical 11 o'clock program. I've been thinking that I might make some new friends if I mingle with other congregants over homemade pastries and a cup of Swedish gasoline. (The congregation is overwhelmingly Scandinavian.)

Yesterday, while nibbling a slice of apple cake and sipping Gevalia, I met a talkative member who regaled me with amusing stories about his life...and the pleasures of golf. Afterward, I decided to take a walk on the second floor of the church whereupon I noticed a room I had never visited before. I peered through the small glass window of the door and entered. The conference room is large and airy with a distinctive 1950s feel about it: green linoleum floors, pale pine cabinetry, ecclesiastical documents on display in vitrines, and landscape watercolors in faded paints on the walls. There is a large oval table with more than a dozen chairs in the middle of the room. It speaks of a time when the church was filled to the brim with members and business, which is basically the two decades of my youth in this town. Now, the space has a touch of museum-quality about it.

For me the main attraction of this parlor was the large collection of scholarly books lined against a wall. As soon as I entered the room, I put down my handbag and started to investigate the tightly packed volumes in the bookshelf. I spotted a captivating title: *The Secret of Radiant Life* by W.E. Sangster. It was published by Abingdon Press in 1957. I took the book from its place and carried it away to peruse at home.

I am in a reading mood these days of autumnal beauty. More precisely, I am in a *searching* mood. As the brilliant ruby, amber, and tawny leaves fall upon my mother's house and yard this fall 2024, I am searching for some answers about pain, loneliness, loss, love, and growth.

This title by a brilliant Methodist pastor/scholar promises a few compelling insights about living well; I sense revelation in its pages. I learn from W.E. Sangster's bio that he "became world-famous as minister of Westminster Central Hall, great preaching center in the heart of London." His profile further states, "Dr. Sangster, a rare combination of preacher and scholar, bases his conviction that man can at least *strive* to live perfectly on the Bible and on Wesley's doctrine of holiness."

This earnest meditation on what it means to live radiantly has, at the very beginning, a chapter about

Saint Paul. I skim the introduction and immediately delve into Sangster's thinking about Saul of Tarsus, his mystic soul and his passionate walk with the Lord. Oscar and I both revered Paul. However, Oscar's alter-ego, Mercado, has this to say about the apostle in *Blue Antiquity*:

> Along the way, Mercado encountered truly perplexing mysteries, such as the conversion of St. Paul, and tried to reconcile that notion, of faith coming upon one as a bolt of light from heaven, with the earthly explanation that Saul of Tarsus had probably suffered an epileptic fit, as he was thrown from his horse; and that he had converted simply to escape persecution as a Jew.

Whatever the truth about the brilliant iconoclast Saint Paul, we both found his story unbelievably mystical. We marveled at the power of it, which brings to mind a beautiful trip we made in the summer of 2013.

A few months before Oscar died, we went to Greece and Turkey to do some research for several writing projects, most notably *Blue Antiquity* for Oscar and my third novel, *A Stitch in Air.* The high point of the trip was our day-long visit to Ephesus. Oscar had been in that ancient site decades previously and always talked about his experience there with reverence, particularly because it is thought that Mary, the mother of Jesus, died on the outskirts of the ancient city in a small cave-like abode, which today is a shrine for Christians and academics alike. I thought it would be a nice surprise to take Oscar to the holy landmark again, so I had arranged for the journey on the sly. I had contacted a travel agent who specialized in tours of Turkish archaeological ruins and booked a flight to and from Ephesus from Istanbul, where we were staying for most of the trip. Additionally, I hired a knowledgeable guide to take us on a jaunt of the ongoing excavations of the great Roman stronghold. When the morning came for the escapade, I explained to Oscar—over a bountiful and delectable Turkish breakfast of flaky white cheese pastries, honey-lacquered fruits, and rich black coffee—what we were about to do. He was beside himself, so thrilled was he at the prospect of the visit.

Most memorable about our gorgeous day in Ephesus was this: Oscar decided to walk around the amphitheater where Paul preached to the Ephesians. He was wearing a beige safari hat because the sun was so brutal, and if I close my eyes this very minute, I can see the exact, sweet expression of wonderment on his face as he took in the history, symbolism, and monumental significance of standing in the same spot where the scholar/apostle Paul had stood to preach the word of God some 2,000 years ago. The memory of it is almost too much for me. I feel my throat tighten; my eyes begin to water.

Is this the radiant life? A life where such deep understanding of being—what *really* fuels the flesh and mind—meets the hem of heaven?

I really can't say. But I do know this: The volume I am holding in my hands by W.E. Sangster is exactly the kind of book that I would have read aloud to Oscar as I savored its wisdom and enchanting stories. I might have eagerly shared the following:

> A little évacué from East London was sent in September, 1939, to a seaside resort on the South Coast. He rose early the next morning and set out for his first glimpse of the sea. Not knowing just where it was, he asked a passer-by.
>
> "Straight ahead!" she said. "Straight ahead!"
>
> The little fellow hurried off again, and then a dark thought crossed his mind. He ran back to the lady who had directed him and said: "Is it free?"

Surely this book that I am loving is one that Oscar would have lifted from my desk upon spying it, claiming rights to read it for "just a few hours while you're running errands, Pupsie." He would have had a huge grin on his adorable face, a naughty glint in his eye, as he quickly made off with this 1957 gem, assuring me, "I'll give it back to you by the end of day, my love. I promise."

Postlude

It is Lent. This ecclesiastical season, a time to dwell on repentance and personal discipline, is about taking stock. A time for "introspection," which was one of Oscar's favorite words. It is also about renewal.

Spring has bestowed its incipient glow on Jamestown, and everywhere I go people are smiling as they remark, "We have sun, we finally have sun." There is veritable happiness in this thawing terrain of western New York, even though the world, with its wars and ravaged people, seems overwhelmingly bleak and hostile.

It is an in-between time for me as I finish this book and reflect upon the last two years of living in my hometown. A very dear pal of mine, a true best friend, unexpectedly died a week ago and my constant rumination of our lifelong friendship has added to the ponderance of this moment. In reflecting on her life with her devoted husband, John, I realize that her marriage and mine were foundational marriages, the kind which serve and nourish, sustain and empower. What I find interesting, though, is that almost nothing about our marriages was similar in nature except for their rock-solid character. That "shared vision" element is what gave our marriages their longevity.

I realize that a marriage such as mine with Oscar will never end. It has changed shape and character, now that he is gone, but it endures. It simply has a hold on me. I guess it's because I married my *soulmate*.

Until now I very matter-of-factly used this figure of speech to describe how I felt about Oscar, but I think I must demand of myself a clear understanding of what it meant to have a soulmate in my husband. I want to be precise.

If I think about the attributes of Oscar's nature, the fact that he was incredibly bold and aspirational, child-like, curious, passionate, garrulous, driven, spiritual and Catholic in tone, social, intellectual, hyper-creative, vibrant-buoyant, musical, reverent, gentlemanly, protective, sweet and open, introspective, compassionate, generous, playful, witty, articulate...there would be one above all others that is salient for me: He was the unseen outline within which I fit perfectly. A human design made just for my being, divinely bespoke, that elevated my nature and brought me closer to eternity.

Acknowledgments

I WOULD LIKE TO NAME CERTAIN FRIENDS who made a true difference in Oscar's and my private life. Many of these individuals have passed away, but while they lived on this earth they enhanced our journey and blessed us, and they are very much a part of my life in memory still: singular scholars Richard Muller-Thym and his wife, Helen Sprinkle, amazing adventurers of so many worlds; one of a kind—sensitive, giving—art dealer/psychoanalyst Jeffrey Hoffeld and his Monet-beautiful editor wife Carol Fein Hoffeld; distinguished diplomats Ralph Zacklin and his precious better-half (*amiga de corazón*) Lyda Aponte de Zacklin; sterling educator Bobby Oyama; Terri Cohen (honey bee); excellent raconteur Bruce Provinzano; humanists/hosts extraordinaire Victor and Virginia Cruz (the best cooks and the most generous, over-the-top hosts I have known); extraordinary playwright August Wilson and stellar costume designer, Constanza Romero; dapper journalist/memoirist Gay

Talese and sophisticated editor/publisher Nan Talese; dashing play-wright John Guare and his distinguished scholar wife/former American Academy in Rome president Adele Chatfield-Taylor (Adele, I truly *treasure* you!); musicians/artists extraordinaire Lou Reed and Laurie Anderson; brilliant composer/conductor Arturo O'Farrill and his accomplished pianist wife Alison Deane; the one and only composer/conductor Chico O'Farrill and his ebullient, force-of-life wife Lupe O'Farrill; salt-of-the-earth novelist Peter Straub and his joyous educator/entrepreneur wife Susan Straub; marvelous scholars/writers Philip Graham and Alma Gottlieb, forever good-hearted and creative Mark McIntyre and Meg Hartigan, daring wordsmith Richard Price; vibrant artist Judy Hudson; singular novelist Paul Auster and his equally accomplished, elegant novelist wife Siri Husvedt (Siri, I remember so many nods of understanding through the years). We loved this circle of creative pals. In addition, I thank our Killam's Point community, our neighbors in that piece of heaven who truly lifted our hearts and brought us so much joy: Bob and Martha Rice and their son Tim, Karen Hibbs and Pete Burton, Susan Bennitt and Claire Bennitt, Prim, Bob, Dana, and Rachel, Bruce and Susan Ackerman, Peter and Katherine Jackson and family, Mike Rosenthal and family—(oh, Mike, may you rest in peace! How I miss our chats on the terrace of your exquisite home overlooking your paradise garden).

Certain precious friends in my life helped me through the writing of this book, too. And I wish to thank them for their faith in me: Cristina La Porta, Marilu Ramirez, Marjorie Agosín, Karen Braziller, John Giachetti, Rita Delespara, Nana Hagouel, Ellen Barclay, and Andy Señor, Jr.

Last but certainly not least, I express my gratitude to my loving and beautiful family: my mother, Marie Carlson, and my late father, Robert V. Carlson, my sister, Leigh Ann Brattain, and brother-in-law, Larry Brattain, and my nephew, Matthew Hijuelos, and his wife, Danielle Hijuelos; my protective and inventive agent Jennifer Lyons (thank you for so much kindness, generosity, and emotional largesse in the truly toughest of times); and my truly visionary, intelligent editor Gretchen Young. Mil gracias, Gretchen! I also wish to express my profound gratitude to Caitlin Burdette and the entire production team at Post Hill Press/Regalo Press. Her team has been exceptional in every way. Additionally, I thank Carisa Hays, my publicist, who has brought so much joy to me in the post-writing journey. Finally, the community of First Lutheran Church in Jamestown, New York, with special thanks to Pastor Mark Swanson (now pastor of St. Paul's in Ellicottville, NY), office manager Liz Lobb, sexton Mike Key, librarian Wendy Larson, and council member Karen Linn.

Thank you, thank you to everyone, for your love, generosity, and prayers.

I would be remiss if I did not acknowledge certain spiritual leaders who have profoundly influenced me. The late, great Dr. Wilton E. Bergstrand (my childhood Lutheran pastor who inventively taught me that God is always on the throne and to whom I owe my interest in the passion story), the late Dr. William Sloane Coffin (a stunning, intellectual titan who opened my adult mind to the majesty and variety of Christianity's message each Sunday at The Riverside Church), Dr. James Forbes (a man of such soulful clarity that he led me forward each

Sunday at the Riverside Church to meet middle-age's challenges with joy), and, finally, a minister whom I have never met in person, the gifted Protestant preacher Joel Osteen. A few words about Pastor Osteen. First, I have *never* been one to watch or pay attention to televangelists, especially those who preach along charismatic lines. So, it is surprising to me that I have found him, and I imagine it is equally surprising to my friends and family.

How did I connect with this powerful preacher whose traditions are different from my own? One Sunday morning, while I was slogging through my husband's vast archives, I turned on the TV for some distraction. I was at a very low ebb; there was a lot of emotional material in those archives for me to digest. Material that could bring me to tears. As I switched channels, I came upon Mr. Osteen delivering a sermon in his monumental Houston-based church. I thought: *Well, why not listen for a bit?* I intended to watch a few minutes and then turn my TV off...but I ended up listening to his entire sermon because it was so consummately delivered and uplifting. And then, after that morning, I started watching Joel on my computer at various moments of the day while working on Oscar's papers. I was always alone, and I found that his messages blunted my loneliness. More importantly, his ability to share hope through the message of the resurrection truly helped me find a way out of my stubborn mourning. He resuscitated my sense of thankfulness...in the throes of pain. His kind, open visage, his compassion, and his refreshing discernment of familiar biblical tales have been invaluable to me.

For these inspired ministers who have touched my heart, I am forever grateful.

About the Authors

LORI CARLSON-HIJUELOS IS AN EDITOR, translator, and writer whose career began at the Americas Society in New York City. She is the anthologist of many books, most notable among them *Cool Salsa* and *Red Hot Salsa*. She is also the author of three novels, including *The Sunday Tertulia*.

OSCAR HIJUELOS WAS ONE OF AMERICA'S finest novelists of the late 20th century. He was the first American of Latino ethnicity, specifically Cuban-American, to win the Pulitzer Prize for Fiction for his beloved novel, *The Mambo Kings Play Songs of Love*. Among his other works is his acclaimed *Mr. Ives' Christmas*, which reveals his Christian faith in the tradition of Catholicism.